D1374160

ME MYSELF & HIM

Books Coauthored by Chris Tebbetts

M or F?

Public School Superhero

Middle School Series

Stranded Trilogies

The Viking Series

Visit us on the Web! GetUnderlined.com

Educators and librarians, for a variety of teaching tools, visit us at RHTeachersLibrarians.com

Library of Congress Cataloging-in-Publication Data is available upon request.
ISBN 978-1-5247-1522-9 (hardcover)
ISBN 978-1-5247-1524-3 (glb.)
ISBN 978-1-5247-1523-6 (ebook)

The text of this book is set in 11-point Optima, 11.5-point Adobe Caslon Pro, and 11.5-point ITC Novarese Pro.
Interior design by Betty Lew

Printed in the United States of America
10 9 8 7 6 5 4 3 2 1
First Edition

ME
MYSELF
& HIM

CHRIS TEBBETTS

Delacorte Press

For Howard

12:30?

The last thing I remember is sucking down a lungful of gas and closing my eyes. My friend Wexler tells me that I set down the cartridge, stood up again, paused like I wasn't going anywhere, and then fell over, almost slow motion, like a tree going down, until I landed face-first on the cement.

All of that's blank in my memory.

When I woke up, if that's what you can call it, the first thing I saw were these yellow and blue streaks, moving away from me like paint running down a windshield. On the other side of that, I saw one of Wexler's black Keens, the ones he wore at the restaurant, but just one of them, right there in front of my face.

"Hang on, man. You're going to be okay. I called the ambulance. It's okay."

It wasn't, though. I could see the shoe, and I heard Wexler's voice, but they weren't, at that time, Wexler's shoe and Wexler's voice. They were just shoe and voice. I had no idea where I was, or how I'd gotten there, or why everything was sideways.

The first thing that kind of made sense was the sound of the siren. I knew it was an ambulance. That was good. At least I knew something.

And then there were all these people. EMTs and police. More shoes.

A cop kneeled down next to me. It was starting to come together.

"What's your name, son?"

I tried to answer, but everything came out g, l, a, and r. "Glaaarh . . . gharr . . ."

"Your name?"

The first words I actually managed were "I'm having . . . trouble . . . speaking."

He just shrugged and took his lack of grasp for the obvious somewhere else. I heard Wexler giving them my information. Then they put a big thick collar around my neck and lifted me onto a stretcher.

The back of the ambulance was like this lit portal with night all around it, and I slid right in. My face didn't hurt. I don't know why, it just didn't. I thought the collar was a bit much, but someone took my hand away when I tried to loosen it.

And then we were moving.

I'd always wanted to ride in an ambulance. It was on the list with helicopter, glider, and, yes, fire truck, so I couldn't help at least noticing that it was happening. The whole thing was so much like a movie or TV show that reality kind of got drowned out. "Riding in an ambulance" was all front and center. "I am so screwed" wouldn't show up for another forty-five minutes or so.

At the emergency room, they wheeled me right in. A doctor came into the bay where they had stuck me and felt around on my face. When she got to my nose, she made this sympathetic kind of sucking sound.

"What happened to you?" she said.

"Well . . ." I didn't know how to tell her anything but the truth. "I did a hit of nitrous oxide and passed out on the cement." My voice was really small, like if I barely said it, it would barely be true. "Does my mom have to know about that?"

"You're eighteen," she said, with the same kind of tone she might use to say *You're a dumbass kid in every respect but the law.* "That part's up to you."

I'm not sure how the standard exam is supposed to go in these situations, but I'm pretty sure I got the discount package after that. She gave me another quick once-over, said something about X-rays, and left.

I lay there alone for a while, and the shame started to creep in, but also a dose of aggravation with myself. Why couldn't I have just said I fell down on the cement?

1:15

Wexler came in a little later. He was still wearing his uniform, minus the bow tie.

"How's it going?" He cupped my hand, just for a second. "Does it hurt?" He was smiling, too, like he was in on the joke, which basically he was. He knew it wasn't funny, and I knew it wasn't funny; but still, it was kind of funny. Wexler was like my lifeline that night.

"You scared the crap out of me, man," he said.

"Did anyone else see it?"

"Nah," he said. "Everyone else was gone. I called nine-one-one, waited with you, gave them your info—"

"Thanks."

"—and, um . . ."

"What?"

"I called your mom, too."

I closed my eyes. Of course he called my mom. I'd do the same thing. Not if it was just some basic accident, but with police and an ambulance and all? Yeah.

"Sorry," he said.

"No," I told him. "It's not like I'm going hide this from her."

"Have you seen your face?" He was smiling again, and I could tell he hoped the answer was no, so he could be the first one to show me.

"Not yet."

"Here." He found a pink plastic mirror, the little-girl kind. I had no idea where it came from, and I wondered for one weird little moment, *Did some girl die in here?*

And then I saw myself. My hair in front was standing straight up, and there were stripes of dried blood from my upper lip to my forehead. My nose had a little quarter-inch gash on the side that didn't look like much, and didn't feel like anything. Of course, my nostrils were now completely different sizes.

Wexler knocked my hand away. "Don't mess with it."

"Or what? It's going to stay that way?"

We both laughed—but only until that little blue curtain opened and I saw my mom standing there.

"Oh, Jesus." She looked pretty much like someone who had gotten a call in the middle of the night to come get their kid at the hospital. It was maybe two in the morning by now. "What happened to you?"

She came over and put a hand on my cheek. Wexler looked around like he didn't know where to be anymore.

And I looked up into her eyes, and I said, "I fell down on the cement."

Chapter 1

11:11

When I woke up the next morning, my clock said 11:11. That meant Mom was long gone to work, and I had the house to myself.

I lay there for a while, piecing it all together.

The strange part was how nothing hurt. I kept touching my nose and honking it back and forth, trying to get some kind of pain out of it, but nothing came. It seemed wrong, somehow—not just physically, but theoretically. I mean, when you fall down on your face huffing whippets in back of the restaurant where you work, it's *supposed* to hurt. You'd think.

More than anything, I felt relieved. It seemed like the worst of this could be behind me, as long as Mom never found out what happened. I didn't like lying to her, but it was done now. I wasn't about to start undoing it.

In fact, I wouldn't have to. Someone else was about to do it for me.

In two hours, Rita Neemeyer was going to come over to

Mom's desk at their real estate agency and say she wasn't sure she should be butting in like this but thought maybe it was better to say something than not say something, just in case. And Mom would ask Rita what she was talking about, and Rita would ask Mom if she'd seen the paper that day. Then she'd put it down in front of her, opened to a small story on page 3, circled in blue pen.

WHIPPED CREAM NOT UP TO SNUFF
Green River—June 24—A young Green River man found there's more than just whipped cream in those cans when he sustained a broken nose

Technically, that's a lie. I didn't actually break my nose, and the hospital said so.

after inhaling too much of the gas inside. Chris Schweitzer, 18, was treated and released at Richmond County hospital after he fell in the parking lot of Smiley's Restaurant, where he is employed. Smiley's management was not immediately available for comment.

I have no idea how that story made its way into the paper, or which reporter was just enough of an insomniac to have somehow picked up on it in the middle of the night. All I know for sure is that it happened.

I imagine Mom sitting at her desk and reading it, all calm on the outside while someone holds an X-ray up to her head, where you can see the little mushroom cloud going off inside.

She wouldn't say anything, though. She'd wait until she was alone again and then hunt me down on the phone, so she could be exactly as pissed off as she didn't want Rita to see her being.

That would come around one-fifteen, but right now it was just after eleven, and I was feeling like I'd dodged a major bullet.

I took my time getting up, and called Wexler. He was in his car and said I should meet him and Anna at the platform. I told him Mom had gone out and gotten cinnamon rolls that morning, and they should get the coffee. They knew how I liked mine.

12:00

I don't know what the platform used to be. Now it's just four wooden legs and a bunch of boards about three feet off the ground, in the middle of the golf course. And we call it the golf course, but it isn't one, and never was. It's just this wide-open space in the middle of our town that they keep mowed, like it's the place you'd go if you wanted to drive some balls (which I've never seen anyone do).

Anna got up on her knees when she saw me coming. She made the same sucking sound the doctor had made, and her hands floated up at her sides like little wings.

"Does it hurt?"

I shook my head. "You should feel inside." I put down the

cinnamon rolls and stuck my two pointers in my nostrils to show her. One went straight up, the other went in at a forty-five-degree angle.

"No. Way." She already had her two fingers pointed up and ready.

"Hold." Wexler leaned in and took the food out of range. "Okay, go ahead." He's funny about stuff like that.

So is Anna, but in the opposite way. She went right for it and put both pointers inside my nostrils, felt around for a second, and then wiped her fingers off on my shorts. "And it doesn't hurt? How is that possible?"

"Physically? Or theoretically?"

I think she thought I was joking, and turned away from me toward the food. I always hated that—losing her attention. Wexler held on to the bag and handed her a roll to keep her nose-fresh fingers out, and I took one, too.

After that, Wexler and I spent a little time getting our stories straight and making sure Anna knew what we were going to tell anyone who asked—that I tripped over a milk crate, passed out, and didn't wake up until the ambulance got there. End of story. It didn't seem that complicated actually, and pretty soon we were back to hanging out in the sun, doing nothing, and having exactly the kind of day I was hoping we could have all summer long.

So when my phone rang, I didn't even bother to pull it out of my pocket. There was nobody I felt like talking to anyway. But then, about thirty seconds later, Wex's phone rang, too, and everything changed again.

He took it out, looked at it, and looked right back up at me.

"Schweitz," he said. "It's your mom."

5:30

Mom's phone call was bad, but the scene at home later was much worse. She used the word *disappointed* at least three times, and asked a lot—*a lot*—of questions, especially about "what else I'd tried" and how I'd "gotten started." It only got more complicated from there.

	The truth	What I told her
What I'd tried	Pot and beer, a few times. Vodka twice (liked it). Tequila once (hated it).	"I tried beer at a party once, and I didn't like it. Last night was just a stupid, one-time thing."
How I got started	My brother and sister made a little project out of me when they were home two Christmases ago.	"You know, just the usual, friends and stuff. But not Wexler or Anna. They've never tried anything."

That last part about Wexler shows you exactly the kind of liar I am, given that (duh) he'd been with me when this happened.

Mom just looked sad. "I don't know, Chris," she said. "I'm not sure what to believe anymore." Then she turned and walked away from me, which was the worst part.

The thing with my mom is, she's been with a lot of liars, including my father, and the one thing I'd always felt like I could do for her was to not be one, too. Now I'd blown even that (= guilt). (And for the record, it's not like Mom has had so many boyfriends; it's just that the liar to non-liar ratio has been, basically, something to zero.)

A second later, she came back in with the phone, hit the redial button, and handed it to me. That could only mean one thing.

"You already talked to him?" I asked, incredulous. "How did you get him to answer at work?"

And then he was there.

"Chris?"

As soon as I heard his voice, I tried to put the phone back in Mom's hand, because I had nothing to say.

"Chris?"

She took the phone then. "Mark, it's me. He's just standing here. Yeah. Yeah. Okay." She put the handset on speaker and set it down on the table. "Go ahead."

"Chris, it's Dad."

No kidding.

"Listen, I'm really glad you're okay. I've already talked to Mom about all this, and I don't think you're going to like what I have to say. I'm just going to lay it out for you. Are you listening?"

My stomach felt like a fist.

"He's here," Mom said.

"You're either going to come here and live with us for the summer, successfully, by my rules, or you're going to pay your own way in the fall."

Giant bomb, hitting the town. Buildings, falling over. Lives, ruined.

"That's it?" All of a sudden I was talking to him. "Just like that?"

"College is a privilege, Chris. It shouldn't be, but it is. So yes, just like that. I'm more than happy to pay for your education, you know that, but after last night, I'm going to need some assurance that this is a good investment."

That statement says a lot about my father. I know that he knows I'm a human being, but I think I'm also like a point on a graph to him, where graph = life. One axis is Time, the other is The Realization of My Potential, as defined by him, and I rise and fall with every accomplishment and every screwup.

"I've got you on a flight Sunday morning. Nothing direct. You'll have to change in Chicago," he said. Like that was the part that mattered.

"God, Dad, can you at least give me a second to think about this?"

"Really, Chris? You really need to think about it? I know this is sudden, but I don't imagine you're going to give up four years at Birch College for one summer of . . . whatever you've been doing so far."

I hate you. I fucking. Hate you.

"What are you talking about?" I asked. "I'm already in. I registered for classes."

Birch had been my first choice, and against all odds, not to mention my own expectations, I'd gotten in, as a film and English double major. I had no idea what I wanted to do yet (as in, when I grew up), but I knew exactly where I wanted to be for the next four years—at Birch. And, just as important, anywhere but Green River, Ohio.

I couldn't not go to Birch, and Dad knew that, didn't he?

"I know you feel forced right now," he said. "I'd feel the same way. But this is all about choices *you've* made. You do understand that, don't you?"

This is what I'm talking about with him. It's like falling down a hole and there's nothing to grab on to because it's all lined with that stainless steel logic of his.

"Just . . . send me the flight information," I said. And then I hung up, because what was the point? I could fight it, or I could give in. Either way, I was going down, and nothing I did or said now was going to make that not be true.

Chapter One

11:11

It was 11:11 when I woke up that morning. I remember, because there are certain numbers I always notice on the clock.

12:12	2:22	4:44	10:11
12:34	2:34	4:56	11:11
1:11	3:33	5:55	11:12
1:23	3:45	10:10	

It's kind of stupid, but for me, they're like miniature good luck when you catch them; like this was the smallest possible way to start the day off right after a night like the one I'd had.

I lay there in bed, replaying everything that had happened, or at least everything I could remember. I remembered the waking-up part, all sideways on the cement, and the police, and Wexler, and Mom. But not the passing out.

After a while, I got up and looked at myself in the mirror.

I had a bruise over my right eye that I hadn't seen earlier, and my nose had the same miniature gash from the night before. It looked like I'd been in a fight, which I'd never, ever been. I stared for a long time, fascinated by my own image. But then I thought of Mom again, and about how she'd hate that this was my reaction. Although only if she knew the truth. Which she didn't.

This was getting complicated already.

I could feel it. The lie had legs.

I didn't want to think about it, so I went downstairs and called Wexler. He was in his car and said I should meet him and Anna at the platform. I said Mom had gotten cinnamon rolls and they should pick up the coffee.

Cinnamon rolls. Yeah. When they're good, I love them as much as it's possible to love food. Which Mom knew. She'd gone out of her way and bought them for me with this whole movie in her head about what had happened the night before. So now they were just sitting there like a big bag of guilt on the kitchen counter. I told myself I wasn't even going to eat them. I'd just give them to Wexler and Anna.

But that was a lie, too.

12:00

Wexler and Anna were already laying out when I got there. I liked that neither of them made a big deal out of my nose, although Anna did feel around inside it, to see how crazy out of shape it was. She never gets grossed out about anything.

"We should get our stories straight," Wexler said. "I already talked to Sheila, and as far as she knows, we were hanging out and you tripped. Period."

Sheila was the manager at Smiley's, and cool, but probably not *that* cool. I wondered if there was still blood on the cement where I fell.

"I'm supposed to work tonight."

"She's covering your shift." Wexler pointed at my nose. "No one wants to order food from that."

"Thanks. Again."

We hadn't even discussed whether or not we were going to tell Anna. It would have been impossible not to.

"So that's it, then," I said. "No one else knows, no one else finds out." I was saying it more for myself than for them. They knew.

It was weird to imagine that three months from now, we'd be scattered in all different directions. I was going to Birch College in North Carolina, Wexler was headed to Ohio State, and Anna was going to BU in Boston. It seemed too far off to be true yet, like a different kind of lie. Too early to be sad, anyway, with the whole summer stretched out in front of us.

So I lay back, closed my eyes, and let the day bake me like everything was normal. Which I guess it was, except that I kept reaching up and touching my nose and wondering if it was ever going to start hurting.

1:11

When I got bored, I turned on my camera and started shooting, like I do anytime I get bored. Anna's eyes were closed, and the sun on her face flared the details a little. I liked the effect.

"What are you going to miss when you go away?" I asked, still recording.

"You," she said.

"Seriously," I said.

"I am serious," she said. "I'm going to miss my mom, and you, and you." She looked over at Wex, and I panned across to him, following her gaze.

"I'm not going to miss anyone," Wexler said.

"Keep telling yourself that," I said. Wex was easily the most sentimental one of us.

"When are you going to show us this thing, anyway?" Anna asked. "This masterpiece?"

"When it's done," I said. "Or before we leave town. Whichever comes first."

I didn't have a specific game plan, but the idea was to make some kind of document (or documentary) of our last summer together, as a kind of going-away present for Wex and Anna. I'd already started picking out music and cutting together some of what I'd shot, starting with graduation.

"What about you, Wex?" I asked, still rolling. "What are you going to miss?"

"This," he said. "Exactly this. Doing nothing, together."

"I'll tell you what I won't miss," Anna said. "This boring-ass town."

"Right?" I said. "Hundred percent. I just want to fast-forward to September."

"Slow down," Wex said. "Don't just wish it all away."

"I'm not," I said. And I really wasn't. I mean, yes, I couldn't wait to put Green River, Ohio, in my rearview mirror, but it was also true that some part of me never wanted that summer—our last two months together—to end.

Both.

6:00

"I want you to call your dad."

That's what Mom said when I walked in the door at the end of the day. She was sitting at the kitchen table with iced tea, and a blank pad and a pencil in front of her, like she'd just made an invisible list, and *Tell Chris to call Dad* was at the top.

"Why?" I said. "Is there an insurance issue or something?"

"No, honey." She said it like it should be obvious, which it was. "It's just not the kind of thing he'd want to hear about at some later date. You went to the emergency room."

My father lived two-thirds of the country away, in California. He's considered brilliant in terms of particle physics—whatever a step down from famous would be—but he basically sucked at being a parent. I always left him as alone as legally possible.

"And I want to be there when you call him," Mom said.

"What?" I stood up, more pissed than I deserved to be. "There's not that much to tell. It was an accident. I tripped."

"You said you fell."

"I tripped and fell, okay?" I hated how hard my heart was beating right now, and how wrong the words sounded to me—so much like a lie.

"It's not like I call Dad every time I go to the doctor," I said. "Seriously, what does this even have to do with him?"

"I just want us all to be on the same page," she said. "That way we don't have anyone wondering later if they got all the information or if there's something more."

There's something more. There's something more. There's something more.

"There's nothing," I said. "Nothing he needs to know. It's all taken care of."

And I could just feel those cinnamon rolls turning into shit in my stomach.

Mom looked at me for a long time, not saying anything. I looked back because I knew I had to.

Finally, I said, "Fine, I'll call him. Just not right now, okay?"

"Okay, but soon," she said.

"I will," I told her. "Soon. I promise."

And then I didn't.

Chapter 2

3:00

Dad was right about one thing: I had to change planes in Chicago.

Usually, I like being up in planes. Your whole life gets put on pause up there, including time. You sit down at 3:00, wait four and a half hours, and when you stand up again, it's 5:30. It's like getting away with something without even trying.

But I wasn't thinking about any of that. I was thinking about everything that had happened in the past forty-eight hours, all the way up to the last fifteen minutes I'd had with Wexler and Anna.

We'd stayed out all night, some of the time with other people but mostly just the three of us. We drove around a lot, not even talking, just listening to music and pretending the whole thing didn't feel like a funeral.

We got breakfast around four, and then at five I finally had to admit that it was time to say goodbye. I was leaving at nine, and Mom, who was already going to be pissed about me staying out, had made me promise it would be just the two of us going to the airport. Also, I hadn't even started packing yet. Hello, denial.

Wexler dropped Anna off first, and I got out to say goodbye. We hugged for a long time on the curb, and I just stayed there, like at some point it was going to feel okay to break apart and get back in the car.

Finally Anna put her hands on my shoulders and turned me around.

"Go. Leave. See if I care."

I kind of hated that she did that, even though I'd probably still be standing there if she hadn't. But it was like confirmation of what I'd always felt, on some level, that even if Anna and I would die for each other, I might die just a little bit more.

Still, I missed her already.

I got back in the car, and held my hand up against the glass while Wexler pulled away. Anna looked down at her phone and then back, and nodded, and I realized she'd thought I was saying something about "five," like *Wow, I can't believe we stayed out this late!* Which was too embarrassingly lame a last word for me to not call her.

"I was waving goodbye," I told her.

"I know, idiot. I love you."

"I love you too," I said, and then forced myself to hang up first.

Neither of us, Wexler or I, said much of anything on the way to my house. He just silently sped through town, given that the streets were deserted at that hour, not to mention Wex's *no cop, no stop* approach to life.

It was just getting light out, and I could see the outline of the water tower at Brandt Park. There was a cool, low-hanging mist in the cornfields along Route 34, and I realized how much I was going to miss all this stuff that had bored me to death for the past eighteen years.

On the other side of my mind, things were a lot more hectic. I was depressed and pissed, and jealous of Anna and Wexler for getting the summer I wanted to have, and for having it without me. I was also incredibly sad, not just for myself but for all three of us at the same time. We were like a triangle. Take one away and all you have is an angle.

Actually, not even, I realized. Just a straight line between two points.

And then we were coming around the corner onto my street, and I don't know why, but something made me ask:

"Are you going to fuck Anna?"

It was like the thought just showed up in my head fully formed. I went from not thinking about it at all to thinking it was probably going to happen in one tiny step, or giant step, I don't know which.

"What are you talking about?" Wexler said. "No." And then again. *"No."*

"I wouldn't want you to, but I wouldn't tell you not to, either."

"Schweitz—"

"I'm just being honest," I said.

"It's not going to happen," Wexler said. "And even if it did, we'd both totally talk to you first. You know that, right?"

I got caught on the logic. If it *did* happen, they'd talk to me *first*?

Then a few more circuits fired, and I'm thinking *did* it happen?

And then I'm thinking *yes*.

Meanwhile, about half a second has gone by in the car.

They say you can withhold bleeding if you don't know you're cut. Then, as soon as you see the slice, or puncture, or whatever, there's no way to stop it. I felt like I was bleeding all over the car now. Even if none of this was true, it didn't matter because I was already stuck thinking it. (And for the record, it did matter if it was true.)

"Please don't worry about this," Wexler told me.

"I won't," I said automatically. "Sorry."

Wexler shrugged the way he did—not like putting something aside but more like taking it off. He could do that in a way I couldn't. I always felt like the designated douche with him, never letting go of anything.

When he got out of the car to hug me goodbye, he was already welling up. Wexler's not self-conscious about that stuff the way Anna is.

"I love you, Schweitz," he said. I knew he did, but he'd never said it before.

"I love you too," I told him, and made him drive away before I went inside.

That was the last I saw of or spoke to either of them before I left. I wanted to call from the airport, but I knew they'd both be asleep by then.

I thought I'd sleep, too, on the plane, but I didn't. I felt wide, wide, wide, wide awake.

5:30

California—meaning Dad, Felicia, and Violet—welcomed me with literally open arms. It was like they'd practiced on someone else, and now I was this pole they were all hugging in the middle of the airport.

"Welcome to California!" Felicia said, twice. I think she thought I didn't hear her. And she definitely didn't realize the face she made when she saw the little gash on my nose. Her and Dad's wedding was just over a month away, and I wondered if she was already thinking about the pictures we'd be taking that day.

I could see Dad trying not to make a big deal about my face either way. He smiled, but he was watching me more than actually looking at me.

"I guess everything ran on schedule," he said.

And thank god for that, Dad. It would be terrible if my summer didn't start sucking in a timely manner.

"Where's the luggage thing?" I asked, and started walking in the same direction as the other people from the plane.

Dad pulled up alongside me in the terminal and dropped his voice. "Listen," he said. "You can get this attitude out of your system for the next few hours, but at seven-thirty, we're going to talk."

Not seven, not eight, but seven-thirty. It wouldn't have

surprised me if he'd said seven-forty, or eight-oh-five. Everything happens for a reason in Dad's world; it's just that he's the only one who lives there.

"I know you're mad, Chris," he said. "I get that. Of course you are."

"Yes, I'm sure that you get it," I said. "You're a very smart guy."

"My point is, I don't expect you to just put on some kind of happy face," Dad said. "But we're not going to have an infinite adjustment period here, either. Meanwhile, try to bear in mind that Violet had nothing to do with this."

I turned around. She and Felicia were walking behind us.

"I'm sorry about this, Violet," I said. I meant it, too, and not just because the whole thing was kind of awkward and unpleasant. My being here meant she'd have to give up whatever exclusive she had on the house—the good TV, the bathroom, whatever—for the whole summer. I would have hated me, at least a little, if I were her.

She shrugged with one shoulder. "It's okay."

Violet had that summer-after-eighth-grade thing going on, trying to look as much like a high school girl as possible. Her hair was still long, but her mouth was really shiny and I think her eye makeup was supposed to be "smoky." She also had two new little boobs, the kind that look like they don't have anything to do with each other yet.

The real thing, though, was how she kept looking at me—like if I came up and ate the fries off her tray in the cafeteria, she might write about it in her diary that night. At first, I felt kind of presumptuous for getting creeped out, but then I looked over at Felicia and I could tell she was seeing it, too.

"Does it hurt?"

Violet was beside me now, and basically looking up my right nostril—the big one—as we walked.

"A little," I said, and chinned over at Dad. "But I've got to get used to him at some point."

"Very funny," Dad said. Violet laughed until she seemed to think she should stop, and then did, really suddenly.

"We're having the pepper steak tonight," Felicia said, also suddenly. "With that marinade you liked so much the last time. And the crème brûlée, with the blueberries?"

It was all very specific—*the* steak, *the* crème brûlée, *the* blueberries. Like it would only ever happen once.

"I'm a vegetarian now," I said.

"Oh. Well—"

"I'm just kidding," I said, but nobody laughed this time.

7:30

The truth is, Felicia's an amazing cook. I hadn't thought about it, but besides September, her food was one thing I could look forward to that summer.

It's not like I thought she and my father didn't love each other, but still, I couldn't imagine looking at Mark Schweitzer and thinking, *yes,* this is the person I want to spend the rest of my life with. Although, to be fair, I can't really imagine falling in love with any of my friends' parents, either. It all seems so particular, like every single one of them was incredibly lucky to have found the other.

Which I guess means we're all extra lucky to even exist. Not only do those two people have to come together at exactly the right time, but then this one sperm out of a hundred million has to get to the head of the line to ensure it's going to be you and not someone else who pops out nine months later. It's like winning Powerball just by being born.

After that, you have to make your own luck, which means sometimes you wind up exactly where you don't want to be, and then your luck is just as bad as it was good a second ago. How many zillions of factors had to line up, how many turned and unturned corners had to be chosen, in exactly the right order, to get me sitting there at my father's dining room table that night, wishing I was anywhere else in the world?

This is the thing.

After we ate, Violet went off to do whatever, and Dad and Felicia asked if I wanted to stay at the table or go sit in the living room instead.

C) None of the above.

"Right here is fine," I said. "Why? What's about to happen?"

Dad clasped his hands and put them on the table, kind of like praying, and kind of like a big double fist.

"Chris, I want you to take some accountability for what happened. I mean, I know that you know what your role in all of this is. Obviously. But I need to see that in you, do you understand?"

"So . . . you want me to act out my thoughts for you?" I said.

In my mind, I gave him the finger.

Then he did this one thing that he and my mom still share. They'll smile in this patronizing way when I'm acting stupider than I actually am. It's a harder habit to break than you might think—for me, I mean.

He took a sip of coffee, to let my stupidity sink in. Then he said, "Actually, I want two things. I want you to speak with a counselor, and I want you to come work at the lab this summer." Felicia moved her head, like maybe an eighth of an inch. "Assuming you're still planning on Birch in the fall," Dad added.

Ladies and gentlemen, welcome to the bottom of the hole. Please remain seated until we've come to a full stop at the terminal and the captain has turned off the HOW DID I NOT SEE THIS ONE COMING? sign.

"What kind of counselor?" I asked.

"Well . . . *drugs*," Dad said. "You're not going to tell me this was the first time you tried anything, are you?"

It wasn't really a question, so I didn't bother answering.

"What does working at the lab have to do with accountability?" I asked instead.

"If nothing else, it lets me keep an eye on you," he said, "until you've shown me you can do it for yourself."

"Oh, because you've been so good at that for the last four years." I couldn't help myself.

"Chris—"

"Doing what at the lab?" I asked.

"Administrative work, mostly. Some data entry, gofer stuff. It's eighteen an hour. I have to imagine that's more than you were making at Smiler's."

At Smiley's, they paid me eight-fifty an hour, plus 40 percent off food, plus whatever I could scarf from the walk-in cooler when no one was around, plus getting to spend my last summer at home with my friends. I'm not sure what that adds up to, but I'm pretty sure it's more than eighteen dollars an hour.

$$(8.50 \times hours) + (food - 40\%) + more food + (home/friends) = ?$$

"Chris, what are you doing here?" Dad said suddenly, and I looked up at him again.

"What am I doing here? Is that a real question?"

"I mean, why do you think you ended up in a place where you're inhaling whatever it was and falling down the way you did? That kind of thing doesn't just happen spontaneously."

"It was pretty spontaneous," I said.

"You know what I mean." He was starting to get mad now. His voice was tightening up. "Stop trying to play the situation. These are honest questions, and I expect sincere answers."

It was like the invitation I didn't know I'd been waiting for.

"You want a sincere response?" I said. "Okay. Fuck you! You're an asshole for bringing me out here. You never had to take care of me before, and you don't even appreciate it. The only time it *finally* comes up is when you—*you*—have something at stake. What's Birch up to now? Sixty thousand a year?"

Dad batted a glass off the table. It hit the wall, and water and ice and pieces of glass spilled down onto the floor.

The first thing I did was look over at Felicia, to see if she was surprised. She was. As far as I knew, this was unprecedented behavior, and she seemed to think so, too.

Dad got up and walked into the kitchen. I didn't think he was coming back, but then he did, with a roll of paper towels and the garbage can. He bent down and started picking the broken glass up off the floor.

"You're going to the office with me tomorrow," he said without looking up. "We leave at seven-forty. Until you're ready to have a real conversation, nothing else is happening."

I took him at his word. If not talking to Dad meant not talking about this at all, then I was all over it. That much, I could live with.

7:42

I spent the rest of the night just hanging out in my room, trying not to boil over again. I'd been in California (= around Dad) for maybe two hours, and already I was turning into someone I didn't want to be. It was a claustrophobic feeling, like getting locked in a closet with my own DNA for two months.

So much for my summer.

And so much for my Untitled Wex-Anna Project, too, I

realized. I only had about two and a half minutes cut together so far, but I spent an hour on my laptop tightening it up, and adding some music. Then I sent it to the two of them, like a token of the much bigger gift I'd had in mind, but oh well.

This is all I got to do. Wish there was more. Enjoy. Love you guys.		

I didn't hear back from either of them right away, so I moved on to my older sister and brother. I just needed to talk to someone—anyone—who had at least a little appreciation for what I was up against out here.

Still, I wish I hadn't gotten Zoey's voice mail, because when I reached David after that, it reminded me why he was the last one I tried. I got about a sentence and a half into telling him what was up before he basically took over the conversation.

"Listen, if you hadn't screwed up, Dad wouldn't be coming down on you like this. That's the bottom line," he said. "And to be honest, I don't know if what happened is a big deal or not, but it is to him. You should take that seriously, for your own good."

David put a lot more stock in Dad than I did. I think he bought into the whole idea that the big career somehow made up for not being a very good father.

"You also broke your nose doing whippets," he went on.

"That's just embarrassing, man. If it were me, I'd say as little as possible and let it go."

"It wasn't broken," I said.

"Not the point."

He didn't give a shit about the whippets, either, though. For him, it was about getting caught. That was my crime. David had been way wilder than me in high school, and he'd gotten away with all of it. Even now, he was waiting tables in Portland and, as far as I knew, still doing his share of late-night partying.

"Yeah, well, I'm paying the price," I said.

"Oh, because living in your famous father's really nice house is such a burden?" he asked. "Is the pool too cold for you?"

"I'm just saying, this was supposed to be my last summer with my friends," I tried again. "I'm allowed to be sorry about that, aren't I?"

"Trust me," David said. "Wexler and whatshername—"

"Anna."

"—aren't going to stay your best friends forever. Give it until Thanksgiving, *maybe* Christmas, but everything's going to change."

"Anyway," I said, because I didn't know where this was going anymore and it hadn't been even a little satisfying, "I'm totally beat. I'm going to go to bed."

Which is exactly what I did next. It was ten o'clock in California by then, which meant one a.m. to my Eastern Standard body, and I had to get up early the next morning for my new job.

Apparently. Now.

Chapter Two

4:35

The back of Smiley's was all rearranged when I got to work that day. The dumpsters were pushed up against the side of the building and there were new shelving units for the milk crates. They also had two big floodlights over the door now, which would do two things: 1) Keep anyone from tripping and falling in the dark, like I supposedly had; and 2) Keep anyone from hanging around back there doing whippets after work, like I actually had.

It was weird, stepping over the spot where I'd been laid out like a corpse the last time I was there. At the same time, I was just a little bit disappointed there weren't any signs of blood. I'd either bled only on myself, or they'd bleached the hell out of the cement in the meantime.

As I stepped inside, I got a very *anything you say* kind of feeling, as in, *can and will be used against you*. That's why I came in late. I was hoping I could just slide in and start working without too much conversation.

The first person I saw was Mitch Mitchell (yes, really),

one of the grill cooks. He was in the back, chopping romaine for Caesar salads.

"You starting or finishing?" I asked.

"Just got here," he said without looking up. The noise was incredibly loud, given that it was just a big knife and a plastic cutting board.

"How's your face?" he asked.

"You tell me," I said.

He stopped for a second, looked, and went back to chopping. "Yep," he said. Whatever that meant. I'd stopped trying to figure Mitch out a long time ago.

"What happened, anyway?" he asked.

"To me?" I asked.

Obviously me, but this was the first time I had to tell my little story to anyone in the outside world, and I was still warming up to it. The trick was to not say too much or too little.

THE STORY	
LIE	TRUTH
I'd been taking out the garbage, when I tripped over a milk crate	I'd been out back doing whippets with Wexler, passed out,
and fell face-first on the cement.	
Wexler came outside looking for me, and when he found me there, passed out,	Wexler puked when he saw my face hit the ground. Then he ran inside and
he called the ambulance.	

— 34 —

"I was taking out the garbage and tripped over a milk crate," I said. The words coming out of my mouth felt just as scripted as they were. "Wexler found me out there and called the ambulance."

"Yeah," Mitch said. "That's about what I thought you were going to say."

"What?"

Mitch was never an easy read, but he'd always seemed essentially benign. Just kind of strange, which was understandable if you believed the rumors about his family, which I actually did. Supposedly, he'd been in some kind of cult with his father in Indiana, and his mom either pulled him out of there herself or hired some guy to go rescue him, depending on who you asked. Either way, Mitch had been living in Green River for about four months now, and that was as much as anyone knew.

To the degree I'd noticed Mitch at all, it was because he seemed to put a lot of energy into not drawing too much attention to himself. The net effect was somewhere along the creepy-weird-shy spectrum, but it was hard to tell where within that to put him.

"Are they firing whoever left the crate outside the door?" Mitch asked.

"What?" I said. "No. I mean . . . I have no idea. I hope not." I hadn't even thought about that. "Why? Was it you?" I asked. Because I'm a terrible person.

"Nope," Mitch said, his eyes still down, but with a little smile that could have meant anything. Like, for instance, that he didn't believe a word I was saying.

"Don't worry about it," he added. "We're good."

The problem being, it felt like he was saying just the opposite.

"What do you mean?" I asked. When he didn't answer, I had to fight to keep from repeating myself while the kitchen resonated with that piercing chopping sound, like some amped-up version of the tell-tale heart.

What do you mean, Mitch?

Chop-CHOP, chop-CHOP, chop-CHOP

What do you mean—

Chop-CHOP, chop-CHOP, chop-CHOP

What do you—

"Hey, Chris?"

I turned around and Sheila was leaning out of her office.

"Good, you're here. Talk to you for a second?" she asked.

"Sure," I said, trying to focus through the haze of my own paranoia. "What's up?"

She looked back at me, like if I'd just think about it for any fraction of a second—

"Oh. Right," I said, and followed her inside.

I was glad for any plausible reason to turn away from Mitch, if only because it was all happening too fast to figure out in real time. Still, it felt like I'd dodged more of a boomerang than a bullet. I couldn't say when or if this might circle back on me again, but it bought me some time, anyway.

The manager's office at Smiley's was tiny, and exactly

square, with no windows. I think it had literally been a storage closet at some point.

"How are you?" Sheila asked after I sat down.

"I'm fine," I said. "Brain damage was minimal."

She smiled awkwardly while my stupid heart sped up all over again. I could still hear the sound of Mitch's knife on the other side of the door.

"We've got an adjuster coming in to talk to you later this week," Sheila said. "You're eighteen, so it's up to you, but your mom can be here too, if you want."

"An *adjuster*?" All I could think of was a chiropractor, which definitely wasn't right.

"Insurance," Sheila said. "There've been a few incidents at other branches, with the lighting in the back. They just want to get your story down and nip this in the bud if they can."

"Nip . . . *what* in the bud?" I asked.

"You know what? I'm not really supposed to talk about it. Actually"—she made a flip-flop gesture with her hands—"I'm really *not* supposed to talk about it. They were hoping to have someone here today, but there was some kind of mix-up. Can you come in on Friday at three?"

Before anything else could happen, the little clock on her desk clicked over another minute, to 4:44. It wasn't much, but it seemed like a good sign.

"Sure," I told her. "No problem."

12:20

I could hear the TV in Mom's room when I came home. That didn't mean she was awake, but it didn't mean she wasn't, either. I tried to walk by her door as quietly as possible.

Then the sound muted. "Chrissy?"

When I leaned in, she was sitting up with the light on.

The bed was the same one she and my father had shared in the old house, but it took up almost the whole room here. Mom always looked so tiny to me in that bed. So alone.

"How was work?"

"Really busy" was all I said, which was true. I hadn't gone back to Mitch with any of what had happened, partly because he was on grill and I was on fountain all night, but more because I didn't feel like dealing with it.

"Sit down for a second," she said.

I sat on the edge of the mattress, too sticky from work to touch anything else. The TV had an infomercial playing for this plant food Mom already had that I think actually worked really well.

"Why are you watching this?" I asked.

"Your father called," she said.

"Oh."

"He wanted to talk to you about the wedding."

"What about it?"

Mom half smiled in this way she has, when it's obvious I'm acting stupider than I am. The topic right now, obviously, was not the fact that Dad and Felicia were getting married that summer. It was the fact that I'd said I would call him after my accident and of course never had.

"What the hell, sweetie?"

"I'm sorry," I told her. "I really was going to call."

Sometime in my life. Like before I died.

"But you didn't," she said.

"I know."

"And you promised me you would."

"*I know.*"

"Do you want me to trust you or not?" Mom said, and I suddenly felt twice as tired as when I'd walked in the door.

I swear, if lying were a job, it would be the equivalent of being one of those giant-headed characters at Disney World. I've heard those people only work something like half an hour at a time, because it's too exhausting to carry around that big fake head for very long.

But the answer was yes, I did want her to trust me. Unlike with my father, I actually cared what Mom thought. She was the one (= only) person who had always been there, and despite appearances, I didn't take that for granted. I really did appreciate it. I just screwed up showing it once in a while.

Or two or three times in a while.

"How much does he know by now?" I asked.

"That you tripped and fell and cut up your face enough to land in the ER, but that you're fine."

"What did he say?" My guess was something like *Thank god for insurance,* or *What time did you finally get home from the hospital?*

— 39 —

"He said you should call him," she said.

And, we're back.

"I will," I said. "I promise, for real. Tomorrow."

"No," she said, almost apologetically, and took the phone off the nightstand. "It's only nine-thirty out there."

I was completely cornered, and didn't even try to find my way out. I owed Mom this much, at least.

"What's his number?" I said. Literally, I couldn't remember the last time I'd called him.

Mom gave me that same half-smile as before, and then hit speed dial—the one I'd kind of forgotten about on purpose—before she handed me the phone.

"Déjà vu," I said.

"What is?"

"Hello?"

It was Felicia who answered.

"Hi, it's Chris," I said.

"*Ohhh, hi*, Chris." Her tone said everything—very sympathetic, very kiss-the-boo-boo. "How are you doing?"

"I'm good," I said.

"Your dad told me you had an accident."

"Yeah."

"But you're okay now?"

"Yeah."

It's not that I disliked Felicia. More like I un-liked her. I just didn't have any like for her. In fact, I didn't have anything for her at all.

Actually, that's not true. I'd always assumed there was

— 40 —

something wrong with her, on some level, if she wanted to spend the rest of her life with my father.

"Is he still at work?" I asked. Like I might be so lucky.

"No, he's right here. Hang on a sec."

I started to get off Mom's bed, and she grabbed my arm.

"Hello?" Dad said.

"It's me, Dad."

"Nice talking to you, Chris."

"Bye, Felicia."

Mom let go at the same moment Felicia clicked off, and I went out into the hall.

"How are you doing?" Dad asked.

"I'm totally fine," I said, and then waited until I'd gone into my room and closed the door. "I think Mom's making too big a deal out of this."

"She didn't make a big deal. She just told me you'd fallen and broken your nose."

"It's not broken. Is that what she said?"

"Maybe not. But that you were in the ER, anyway."

"It's fine now. Really," I said.

"You sure?"

"I'm sure."

"Well, good," Dad said. "Hey, and did she show you that *New York Times* piece from last week?"

"I don't think so," I said, even though she had. It always surprised me how quickly Dad could move the topic over to himself.

"It's an article in the Sunday magazine," Dad went on.

"They profiled my book and called me a 'go-to theorist' in American academics. Not bad, right?"

"Not bad," I said, scratching at a bug bite on my knee. Mosquito? Something else?

"And did I tell you I have a TV agent now?" he went on. "It's kind of ridiculous, but Reuben thinks it's a good idea."

Supposedly, PBS was looking at turning Dad's big best-seller into a series. I had no idea who Reuben was, but I didn't want to ask any questions. Dad's ego was like this stray animal, and the more you fed it, the more it kept coming around.

"Mom said you were calling about something else?" I asked. I seemed to instinctively avoid saying *the wedding* whenever I could. It just felt too weird. Or at least weird enough to avoid.

"Right. I wanted to pin down your travel plans for next month," Dad said.

"When is it, again?" I asked.

He sighed. "Really?"

"July twenty-fifth, right?"

I was standing in the middle of my room, looking at my face in the mirror. There were probably going to be pic-tures at this thing, weren't there?

"I'd like you to come out by the twenty-second, and maybe go back on the twenty-ninth," Dad said. "Unless you'd like to stay longer."

"Well, that's the thing," I said. "I'm not completely sure I'm coming anymore."

"*What?*"

I hadn't planned on saying that. Not yet, anyway. I'd been waiting for the right moment, and this one had come up so suddenly, it was like an on-ramp I had to swerve to catch.

"Everything is so up in the air right now," I told him. "I don't want people to see me like this. Grandma and everyone? It's embarrassing."

"Please don't tell me you're going to use this accident as a reason to stay home four weeks from now," Dad said.

"I'm not," I said.

I was. But I couldn't tell him that.

Meanwhile, the possibility of not going to Dad and Felicia's wedding had blazed to life, and I was flying, moth-like, straight toward it. Just the idea of staying home gave me this warm, irresistible feeling, which if I had to translate into English would be something very close to *Yes*.

Dad hadn't gone as far as asking me to be in the wedding, which I thought was uncharacteristically realistic of him. I assumed David would be best man, but I really didn't know. It would be a good choice, anyway. He'd moved out the same year as Dad and still thought Dad was a great, if misunderstood, guy. Zoey had her share of resentments, but she was very good at keeping them to herself. And I was the difficult one. Not that it was a competition.

Not that it wasn't, entirely, either.

"I mean, I'm not saying I'm not coming," I told him. "It's just hard to know anything at this point. Can we maybe talk about it later?"

Dad sighed, quietly enough so it would seem like he

was hiding it, but loud enough to make sure I knew how difficult I was being. His message was always clear—*I moved on a long time ago. Why can't you?*—even when he didn't know he was sending it.

"Tomorrow?" Dad said.

"I guess—"

"Tomorrow," he said.

"Okay."

"This is important, Chris," he said, because of course

Important to Him = Important

"I understand," I told him. "I'm not trying to be a jerk, Dad."

I didn't have to try. It came naturally.

"I know," he said. "But think carefully about this, okay?"

"I will. Good night," I said.

"Good night," he said, and we hung up.

Yeah, I definitely wasn't going to that wedding.

12:35

I texted my sister as soon as I was off the phone with Dad. I needed a reality check about all this. Mom was another option, but I'd already pissed her off by "forgetting" to call Dad. This wasn't exactly the time to ask her about not going to his wedding.

Hey Zoey! You around?	
	What's up?
How long are you going to be out in CA for Dad's wedding?	
	Thursday to Sunday. I wish it could be longer, but I have to work.
Because I'm actually thinking I might not make it.	
	WHAT?????
Since my accident.	
	What about it?
I look ridiculous.	
	I'm sure you're exaggerating.
Check it out	

I snapped a selfie that, okay, yeah, might have been a little extra-close, a little unflattering on purpose, but it was still an actual picture of my nose.

	It's fine. I can barely tell.
I don't want to hear what Dad has to say about it.	
	Tell me again how this happened??

I tripped on a milk crate at work. Why does that matter?	
	Can't argue with you right now, but don't you dare not come. I'm serious.
I don't know . . .	
	I'M SERIOUS
I heard you the first time. And don't kill me if I don't come.	
	I WILL kill you if you don't come. Seriously, don't blow this off.
It's just something I'm thinking about, okay?	
	Not okay
And please don't say anything to Mom about this	
	Obviously.

12:50

After that, I moved on to Wex and Anna. I couldn't wait to tell them what I'd set in motion, and hopefully get a little more backup about it than I'd gotten from Zoey. But when I tried calling Wex and then texting Anna, he didn't pick up and she didn't answer.

I thought about going back out to see if anyone was around—maybe drive past Eddie's or see if they were out at the platform. That was the idea when I got into the shower anyway, but by the time I got out, I remembered how freaking tired I was. So I just went to bed.

I'd tell them about it later.

Chapter 3

7:40

There was a raging silence in the car on the way to Dad's office that morning. You could just hear us *not* talking all the way there. It was bookended by him saying something like, "Ready to go?" at the house, and then, "Here we are" when we pulled into the parking lot near his building on campus.

He worked in Moore Hall, which was a huge concrete block of a building with long rows of windows that looked black from the outside. It's the kind of place you might see from the highway and think, *Insurance,* or maybe, *Thank god I don't work there.*

When we got to the front door, Dad stopped.

"In here," he said, "you're my employee, and I don't mean that in an oppressive way." He put air quotes around *oppressive.* "I just mean that whatever we have going on out there"—for *out there,* he pointed toward the parking lot and, presumably, the rest of the world—"it needs to stay that way. If we're going to make this work, I'll expect professional behavior from you."

As always with Dad, there was what he said, and then there was what he meant. In other words:

If we	If you
are going to make this work,	want to go anywhere but community college in the fall,
I'll expect professional behavior from you.	don't do or say anything to embarrass me in front of these people, whose opinions I actually care about.

"I hear you," I said, which had some subtext of its own.

I hear you.	I am balancing sincerity with brevity.

The lobby of Moore Hall was as generic as the outside, with fluorescent lights and carpet that was too bland to call gray. It was quiet, too. The summer session hadn't started yet, so everyone was either gone or holed up with their research. In fact, we didn't see anyone at all until we got to the physics department office on the second floor. At the door, Dad gave me one last *here we go* look, and walked in ahead of me.

"Good morning, Gina," he said.

"Good morning, Mark. Morning, Chris," she said.

She was sitting at one of the three desks in the front area, facing the computer with her hands floating over the keyboard like she'd put them on pause. Her skin was pale white, especially next to her hair, which was black-black, and her mouth, which was the color of red ballpoint pen.

And she knew my name.

"No messages," she said, but just to me. Then she winked.

I usually think of winking as this really hokey thing to do, but I gave her a pass on it. She seemed nice. It was almost like some kind of secret hello. I wondered if she knew the story behind the gash on my nose, and I had to resist the itch that sprang up there as soon as I thought about it.

"Chris, you're going to be here," Dad said. He pointed at one of the two empty desks. "I'm sure Gina won't mind helping you get set up."

"Yepper," she said, and smiled again. I couldn't tell if she was twenty-five, or forty, or what. "In fact, let me go steal you a better chair than that. Someone took Billie's about an hour after she went out on maternity. I think it was Tia—of course."

She and Dad said "of course" at the same time, and then laughed on either side of me. By the time I realized I hadn't even said a word yet, Gina was already out the door.

Dad put a hand on my shoulder.

"Born-again Christian," he said. "So take it easy on her."

"What do you mean?" I said.

Dad looked at me like I knew full well what he meant. Which I didn't.

"*Anyway,*" he said. "You'll be working for me, both of my postdocs, Serge and Olivia, the grad team, and any spillover from Mathematics if you have the time. I'd like you to start by going around and introducing yourself to everyone."

I was still stuck on the part from before, so I mostly just heard something, something, something, *I'd like you to start by going around and introducing yourself to everyone.*

He had to be kidding.

"Dad, you've got to be kidding. I just got here."

"Well, exactly."

"What am I supposed to tell people?"

He looked a little sad then, like the plan for having brilliant kids just hadn't worked out the way he'd thought it would.

"That you're my son, and you'll be working in the office for the summer," he said. When I didn't respond, his eyes took a little snapshot of my nose. I'm not even sure he knew he did it. "Just keep it simple," he said. "Not everyone has to know your life story, Chris."

The door opened, and Gina came in pushing a chair on wheels ahead of her. The way she was bent over, I noticed a gold cross I hadn't seen before, dangling just under her chin.

"Catch," she said, and rolled the chair across the floor to me. Dad had to move out of the way, but he didn't seem to mind.

"All right then," he said. "I'm in 234 down the hall if you need me. And I'll have some reports for you to input in a little while. Gina, can you get him set up on Billie's computer?"

"Sure," she told him. And then he was gone. I felt like I'd just been dropped off for the first day of kindergarten.

Gina sat down and swiveled around in her own chair to face me. "Your dad just told me on Friday that you were coming. Was it a last-minute thing?" she asked.

Over her shoulder, I could see she had a tiny framed portrait of Jesus on her desk. He was looking up at something outside of the frame.

"It was, um . . . yeah, a last-minute kind of thing," I said.

"Well, I'm sure you're going to love it here. Like, not *here*." She waved her hands around the office. "But I mean, California. It's great this time of year. And your dad's really easy to work for."

"I passed out doing whippets at my old job," I said, pointing at my nose. "That's why I'm here. Dad wants to keep an eye on me for the summer to see if he still wants to pay for college."

Her face got long. Her chin dropped and her eyebrows notched up.

"I'm supposed to go talk to a drug counselor tonight," I said. "It's all more than a little ridiculous, I know."

Then she smiled and cocked her head. "Are you joking?" she asked. I shook my head, and her face went back to long. "Oh."

I don't know why I told her. Maybe because Dad would hate it. But it also just seemed simpler than making something up, which I would have had to do eventually, since we were coworkers now.

Or at least *for* now.

"What are whippets?" she said.

I hadn't been expecting any questions, but I liked that she

was curious. Maybe it was a Christian thing. Let Jesus do the judging.

"Nitrous oxide," I said. "Laughing gas, like at the dentist? It also comes out of whipped cream cans."

She shrugged. None of it meant anything to her. "So I guess you're not so happy to be here, after all. I'm so sorry this happened to you."

Now I was starting to get uncomfortable. I'd been the master of my own information for about two seconds, but then just as fast, I was turning into some kind of victim, and I didn't know what to say anymore.

"Is there a bathroom around here?" came out.

She smiled, maybe at the question itself.

No. There's no bathroom here.

"Down on the right," she said.

"Thanks. I'll be right, um . . ."

"Take your time," she said, and I got out of there before the weird completely took over.

I walked down the hall, past the bathroom, and into the stairwell. Then I took out my phone and texted Wexler.

Hey	

He was right there.

	Hey! What's going on? We totally miss you.
You won't believe where I am right now	

	Disneyland
No	
	The beach
At my job	

A second later, my phone rang.

"What do you mean, your job?" he asked me. "You just left, like, yesterday."

"Exactly like yesterday," I said.

"What are you doing?"

"Working for my father on campus. I'm supposed to be going around and 'introducing myself' to everyone right now."

"Wow," Wexler said. "So not worth it."

I loved that he knew right away how bad that was.

"Come home to us, Schweitzy," he said. "We miss you."

"What about you guys? What are you doing today?" I asked him.

"Anna's shopping with her mom, but we're going to hang out later."

I couldn't help feeling jealous, of all of it. I hated that he knew where Anna was, and I hated that they'd be on the golf course tonight while I was telling my life to some drug counselor I'd never met before.

I also hated that I hated it. Why couldn't I just be mad instead of being mad at Wexler for being the lucky one? I don't think he had any idea how little I deserved his friendship sometimes, and the fact that he couldn't see it was just one more reason why he was a better friend than me.

"Listen, I'm sorry I was so weird when we said goodbye," I told him.

"Weird about what?" he said.

"You know. About you and Anna."

"Oh," he said. "Don't worry about it. It's not like anything's going to happen."

I wasn't so sure about that. At all. But before I could say anything else, the hall door opened and a guy with a beard and glasses was there.

"Are you Chris?" he said in some kind of accent. Israeli? French?

I nodded. "Wexler, I've got to go. I'll talk to you later."

"When are you going to be around?" he said.

"Five maybe? I have to go."

"Okay. Hey, what time is it there, anyway?"

I'm not sure why some people think *I have to go* means *I have to go in a little while,* but Wexler did that a lot.

"Hanging up now," I said.

"Later."

The guy with the beard was still standing there, waiting. "I'm Serge," he said, and handed me a pocket recorder. "Sorry to interrupt, but can you type these notes up for me?"

"Um." I looked down at the unfamiliar little machine in my hand. And I was thinking, eighteen dollars an hour was pretty good money. It was way more than I would have been making at Smiley's.

But still.

"What time do you need this?" I asked.

— 55 —

5:40

"So overall, how was your first day of work?" Dad asked in the car later.

"To be honest, I don't know how to answer that," I said. "I mean, compared to what?"

He smiled at that.

"Do you think this will get any easier for you?" he asked.

I wasn't sure what to say there, either. We were on our way to meeting my new drug counselor, so technically it was a premature question.

"If it's true that everything gets better with time," I said. "Then yeah, sure."

"Not everything does," Dad said. "In fact, it's arguable that most things don't."

Typical. Where I usually had a hard time lying, Dad had a hard time not telling the truth. It's like we were cousins that way.

"Is there any chance I could go out tonight?" I asked him.

"What do you mean? Out where?" he said.

Out of the house. Out of your immediate vicinity. Out of my mind.

"Like a movie or something," I said. "Just out."

"Well, first of all," Dad said, "we're not even going to be home until seven-thirty and you have to get up for work again tomorrow. But if you're asking about using the car in general, that's a no for the time being. Not this soon. I barely even—"

He stopped whatever he was going to say and looked straight ahead.

"You barely what?" I said.

"It's a little fast," he said. "You haven't even been to your first appointment. I don't know if you have a bigger problem than you're letting on, or not. That's just honest."

I know my dad's a physicist by profession, but he's kind of a mathematician at heart. Mathematicians like unequivocal answers. They like equations they can balance and put in a drawer.

And I can tell you for sure that Dad was waiting to hear from this counselor, whoever she was, so he could know what his opinion about my problem was going to be. In other words, he also knew when to outsource.

"So just for the record, am I going to be allowed to drive at all this summer?" I asked. "I'm not trying to be loaded about it. I'm just asking so I can know."

"Don't box me in, please," Dad said. "Part of that's up to you. I don't object to you using my car in theory—"

In theory.

"—and we can all go to a movie this weekend if you want. But as for solo driving, we're just not there yet, okay?"

"Okay," I said, surrendering more than agreeing. This was actually the best conversation we'd had since I'd gotten to California, which wasn't saying much, except that everything's relative, I guess.

Then Dad's phone dinged.

"Can you check that, please?" he asked.

It was a text from Felicia, but I couldn't see what it said on the lock screen.

"What's your code?" I asked. I wondered if he'd give it to me. And I think, but I'm not sure, that he wondered, too, just long enough for both of us to notice it was happening.

"Three one four one," he said, and I couldn't help smiling.

"Yum," I said as I punched it in. "Pie."

6:54

"Do *you* think you have a problem?"

I took a deep breath; not quite a sigh. More like an ellipsis. When she asked me that question, the first thing that popped into my head was Dad, but I knew that's not what she meant. Right now, Dad was sitting in the waiting area, maybe or maybe not hoping I'd feel guilty for all the time he had to spend away from the lab for this.

I shrugged. "Thinking you don't have a problem is a sign of having one, right?" I said.

"Not necessarily," she said.

Her name was Martina Williams. She ran a private practice in an old converted house with a few other people whose names were all on plaques outside the front door. The office where we were sitting had been somebody's living room once. There was a fireplace that had been bricked up, and I wondered how many fires had ever been built there, seeing as how it never got below fifty degrees in this part of the country.

My mind was wandering.

We'd already talked about what my drinking habits were, what drugs I'd tried, and when I'd started "using." Anything that came to me after a question had gone by, I just let slide. I didn't want to start contradicting myself with two versions of the same story.

When she'd asked me what brought me there today—*So, what brings you here today?*—I'd said, *My father drove me,* and she'd said, *No, I mean—* and I'd told her I knew what she meant, and that my father was making it one of his conditions for paying for college.

Then she'd asked me to go back a step, and that's where she got the whole story about the whippets and my face and all. The bridge of my nose still looked broken—to me, anyway, since I knew what it had been like before. Other than that, though, it just looked like I had a small cut, like maybe someone had stuck the tip of a knife inside my right nostril and given it a flick.

"Have you had any other bad drug experiences?" she asked me.

"Like what?" I asked.

"Anything at all. Something you might regret. Things you've said, or done, or things that have happened to other people you know while you were under the influence."

"Does throwing up tequila count?"

She smiled. "Do you regret it?"

"The tequila, or the throwing up?"

She smiled. "Either."

We talked about Mom and Dad, Felicia, Violet, and even

Wexler and Anna. She asked if I had had any traumatic experiences in my childhood that I still thought about.

I wasn't sure how to answer that one.

"Nothing violent, if that's what you mean."

"Not necessarily," she said. "Anything that makes you uncomfortable when you look back on it."

Again, Dad was the first thing that popped into my head, but I didn't want to play the divorce card here. That had BLAMES OTHERS FOR HIS PROBLEMS written all over it.

At the same time, if she was going to start telling me that Dad walking out on Mom and me was the reason I ended up passing out in the back of Smiley's, I didn't want to hear about that, either. Sometimes you passed out in the back of Smiley's because you passed out in the back of Smiley's.

But she didn't go there. Not out loud, anyway. Finally, she sat up a little straighter, looked at her watch, and took this really obvious breath.

"Okay, here's what I'm hearing from you," she said. "Whatever experiences you've had with drugs and alcohol have been a secret from your parents, up until *that* happened." She motioned at my face, more openly than anyone had up to now except for Wexler and Anna. "And you don't seem to mind that it happened, so much as you mind what's happened as a result. Would you disagree with any of that?"

"I guess not," I said. Was there even time to disagree? Not that I wanted to. Because then I'd have to come up with a reason why, and blah blah exhausting.

"I'd like you to come to a group meeting," she said then, and my heart kind of sank like an old beach ball.

"Group of what?" I said. "Do you have a lot of people with nitrous oxide problems?"

"It's a mixed group," she said, like I'd asked a serious question. "We meet once a week, on Wednesdays at six o'clock . . ."

It was like the verbal version of walking me to the door.

". . . and I prefer a six-meeting commitment from newbies," she said.

Newbies.

"Why?" I said.

"'Why?'"

"What am I supposed to get out of it?"

She smiled and sat back. "College tuition?"

I laughed. She was probably just bullshitting me to get me to play along, but I liked that she said it.

"Do I have to decide right now?" I asked.

"No," she said. "Treatment's always a choice. I mean, except when it's not. But for you, yes."

All these words.

"Treatment for what?" I said.

"Don't get caught on the semantics. Any kind of therapeutic experience comes under the umbrella of treatment," she said, and looked at her watch again. Not that I could blame her. I'd make people leave after an hour of this, too.

"But I don't think it could hurt for you to give this a try," she said.

"Ow . . ." I reached over and grabbed my arm like it hurt.

She laughed. "You're a funny guy," she said, like she meant it, but also USES HUMOR TO SUBSTITUTE FOR REAL FEELINGS.

Then she went into her wrap-up.

"You're eighteen, Chris. It's up to you if you want to do this, and please don't take what I'm about to say as any kind of threat. But here's what I see. Your dad wanted you to talk to me, and he made it a prerequisite for college tuition. Now, if you go out there and tell him you're all done and everything's taken care of, I doubt he's going to buy that. But if you show him you're willing to consider another way—just showing up, and listening—he might get off your back."

It took me a long time to respond. Some part of me already knew I was going to that group meeting, but the rest of me hadn't caught up yet.

"I'll think about it," I told her.

"Okay," she said, and stood up.

I wonder if she believed me.

Chapter Three

11:12

Here's something I didn't see coming: My new nose turned me into a kind of modified vampire. Suddenly, I was a little more at ease being seen in the dark—or at least the dim—than in the light.

So it felt just about right to see all my friends for the first time at the amphitheater that night.

The amphitheater was like the platform, in that it used to be something (in this case, an actual theater), but nobody used it for shows anymore, and everyone hung out there at night. And by everyone, I just mean some people.

Most of my friends were going to college that fall. For me, it was a total given. I knew on some level that it just meant trading one structured existence for another, but I was ready for the change. It was like a skin that wanted to come off. I could feel it, peeling away around the edges. All I'd ever known was this town, these people, this existence. Which wasn't a bad thing, at all. But it *was* just the one thing.

"You know what we should do?" Wexler said before we got inside the amphitheater. "Sleep out in the pine forest tonight."

"I like that," Anna said.

"What about you, Schweitz?" Wexler asked me.

"*Psh*," Anna said, because we were there now, and it went without saying that we weren't going to make this a whole group thing. At a minimum, it made sense to wait and see who else was around to hear us talking about it.

The amphitheater was basically a big concrete bowl. There was still a light booth at the top, but it was empty. And the seats were just rows of concrete steps facing a big curved wall that used to be a backdrop for a stage that wasn't there anymore. Now it was just a place to meet, and hang, and be.

We always hung out around the top rows. It was like junior/senior privilege, since nobody older than us even bothered with that place. Underclassmen (= anyone without a license) were more likely to ride their bikes through in the dark, stage left to right, or right to left, depending on where they were headed, while we sat back and looked down on them. The whole thing was like a high school in microcosm.

Also, no lights.

Berylin came over to say hi first and gave me a big hug that almost knocked me back.

"What's *up*?" she said into my shoulder. "How're we *doing*? I heard you went to the emergency room and *everything*."

"Define 'everything,'" I said.

"Well, just that you tripped on a milk crate and went down *really* hard."

"Yeah," I said.

It only made sense to be consistent with the lie. Telling different things to different people was a recipe for paranoia, if not disaster.

Berylin held her phone up to my nose. "Can I look?"

"Sure," I said, and closed my eyes while she lit up my face with her screen.

"It actually doesn't look that bad, to tell you the truth," she said. Like I'd *want* it to look bad. Which maybe I did. A little bit.

"What was the worst part?" Eddie asked. He handed me a big bag of chips. Salt and vinegar, from the smell.

"Probably waking up and wondering where I was," I said. "Like having amnesia and not knowing if it was going to go away."

"Ew," Anna said.

"Did it hurt?" Eddie asked.

"Not really," I said.

"Really?" Eddie said.

"Does it now?" Berylin asked.

"Not really," I said.

I honestly didn't know whether I liked or disliked the attention more. On the one hand, I kind of wished they'd stop with all the questions. But on the other hand, I wasn't fully ready to let go of the whole *what happened to YOU?* thing. It's like when you've been sick, and someone asks how you're doing, and you say you're feeling better, but you don't mean *all* better. But then it's too late, because you can feel them already moving you into the all-better column, like it or not. I get it, but I don't always like it.

So I was a little bit sorry when Anna changed the subject, even though I'm pretty sure she did it for my sake.

"What were you guys just talking about?" she asked.

"Oh!" Berylin said. "*This.*"

She held out her phone again to show us a black-and-white picture. It was a guy standing in front of a car, in a suit, with the brim of his hat in his teeth. He looked familiar, but I couldn't remember his name. Some black-and-white-movie guy.

"Um . . . okay?" Anna said.

"It's all these last known pictures of famous dead people," Berylin said. "And it kind of tripped me out."

I pulled out my own phone, turned on the camera, and started shooting Berylin's screen while they scrolled through a bunch of others. Elvis Presley was in there, and Bob Marley, and Philip Seymour Hoffman. Mostly men. Wexler lasted the longest before he handed back the phone, where the slideshow had come around to the guy with the hat again.

"Yeah, that's not too depressing," he said, while I kept recording in the dark. I wasn't sure this was anything I could use for my Untitled Wex-Anna Project, but I was liking the conversation. If nothing else, I thought, maybe I could lay the audio over other visuals later.

"It's not *depressing*," Berylin said. "It's just weird. He gets his picture taken, goes inside, and has a heart attack instead of having lunch."

"He did?" I asked.

"I don't know. Or something," Berylin said. "The point is, he had no idea it was the last time he was getting his picture taken."

"Yeah, but so what?" Anna said. "You never know when your last *anything* is."

"Right?" Wexler said, and took a chip out of the bag. "Maybe this is the last chip I'll ever eat."

"Ooh, get a shot of that," Anna said to me, and everyone laughed.

"You know—" I said, but Berylin had already decided to be weirdly offended, and put away her phone.

I was going to say, *You know, if one of us dies in the next twenty-four hours, the rest of us are going to be really freaked out by the fact that we had this conversation.* But I never got the chance.

"She's right, though," Anna said. "It can all just go— *pfft*—at any time. Brain aneurysm. Falling satellite."

"Falling satellite?" Eddie asked.

"She's not talking about likely," I said. "She's just talking about possible."

"Thank you," Anna said.

"I mean, think about it," I said. "Just the existence of an idea makes that thing infinitely more likely to happen than an idea that doesn't exist. It's like taking that falling satellite from zero chance to any chance at all, just by thinking it up in the first place."

"Yeah, I'll have some of what he's smoking," Eddie said.

Anna made a wrong-answer buzzer. "*Ehhh*. Physicist father," she said.

"*Theoretical* physicist father," Wexler said. "Dude, haven't you heard of Mark Schweitzer?"

"Can we talk about something else?" I asked.

It was my own fault, though. I was the one who went there, bringing up one of the very few things I could remember Dad talking about—multiple realities, parallel universes, and all that. The multiverse.

"What was that sound again—*pfft*?" Wexler asked Anna.

"Yep," Anna said. "That's the sound of life coming to an end. Just in case anyone was wondering."

"Got it," he said. "So the end of life sounds like a turtle fart?"

"That's exactly how it sounds."

"Wow, you know a lot," Wexler said. "Hot."

"Isn't it?" she said.

And then Eddie was talking about how badly their beagle always farted, and everyone was laughing again, and my father was officially off the table, along with my nose. Which was fine, because I'd just gotten caught up on something else completely.

This. Since when did Wexler concern himself with Anna's hotness?

It seemed kind of impossible and totally plausible at the same time, that after four years of high school the two of them would suddenly go there in the last summer before college. If that's what was happening.

Maybe it was like gravity, the way it gets stronger as you

get closer to the sun, and the sun was September, when we'd all be heading out of town and not seeing each other anymore. So maybe they thought, *What the hell*, because pretty soon it wouldn't matter. Once you reach the sun, nothing does.

Or maybe it was something more than that. Or less than that.

Really, I had no idea. Which is kind of the point.

12:44

We drove to the edge of the Rambles and parked in a lot they only use once a year, when they're selling Christmas trees out there.

A little farther in, past the tree farm, it was just woods with an old fire road running through it, all the way to the pine forest.

Anna had two sleeping bags and pillows from her house, Wexler had a third sleeping bag, and we had a grocery bag with water, three subs, some grapes that we were just going to risk eating unwashed, and a box of three kinds of doughnuts for the morning, if they lasted that long. I didn't want to go home for any of my stuff, because talking to Mom on the phone was one thing, but something told me if she saw my nose, she was going to remember that she didn't want me sleeping out.

Wexler also brought a flashlight and a tarp so we wouldn't get wet sleeping on the ground. Fire wasn't an option out there. I'm not even a hundred percent sure we were allowed to sleep in the pine forest, but everyone always did.

When we got there, nobody else was around as far as I could tell. Nobody had taken the best spot, anyway.

"I've got to pee," Anna said. "Give me the flashlight."

"Why do you need a flashlight to pee?" Wexler said.

"Because I don't trust you with it when I'm peeing," she said. "Give it."

"Good call," he said, and she went off into the dark.

I thought about saying something to Wexler just then. The question flicked through my mind, for the third time now. *Are you going to fuck Anna?* But it was like a dart I didn't want to throw, because I wasn't sure where it was going to land.

So I just ate my sub instead.

We hung out. We talked. I recorded some more of our conversation in the dark. I was liking this idea now, of mixing dialogue with other images, like a spoken-word montage, if I could pull it off.

We even looked at a couple more of those Last Photo photos, but something told me none of us was going to give Berylin the satisfaction of mentioning it later.

?

I don't know what time I fell asleep. The last I checked it was two-thirty.

And then I was awake again.

It was still pitch-black, and I wasn't sure why I'd just woken up, until I heard them moving around.

It was somewhere off to my left. And even though I couldn't see, I knew Wexler and Anna weren't there on the tarp with me.

For a long time, I just lay still, picking sounds out of the dark. They were being really careful, enough that I couldn't tell what they were doing for sure. The only way for them to have been quieter would have been to do nothing. And they definitely weren't doing that.

Finally, I'd been holding on for so long, I forgot I was doing it. That's when I coughed, and the tiny sounds stopped.

"Chris?" Wexler said, not even whispering. It was like he breathed my name.

"Yeah?" I said.

If I had it to do over again, I would have kept my mouth shut, no question. But life doesn't come with do-overs. As soon as I spoke up, I had to go with it.

"I think I'm going to take off," I said.

"No," Anna said, and sat up. I couldn't see if she was wearing anything; I could barely make out her shape in the dark. Still, I felt like I shouldn't be looking. Which kind of told me everything I needed to know.

"It's not a big deal," I said. "I'll sleep in the car. Wexler, where are your keys?"

"No, no, no, no, no," Anna said. "Don't go."

I wondered if this was their first time. Probably not,

with me right there. Which was worse. It just made whatever I'd been left out of up to now that much bigger.

"Don't worry about it," I said. Making them leave would have added a whole lot of guilty to the already-awkward of the whole thing. "Wexler, I'm going to take your flashlight. You guys both have your phones, right?"

"We'll come, too," he said.

"*No,*" I said, hard enough so it wouldn't sound perfunctory. Or pathetic. "Seriously. I'll sleep in the car."

"No way," Anna said.

"Please?" I said. "It's no big deal."

"Which part?" Anna said.

"Anna," Wexler said. I looked over at Wexler, but mostly just saw the space where I knew he was in the dark.

"I'm going," I said.

"We're all going," Anna said. She was already standing up and pulling down her shirt, I think. Wexler got up, too.

"And I'm really, really sorry, Chris," Anna said.

"Don't be," I said, because that seemed like the right thing to say. So did *You're not the ones who should be sorry.* But I just stuck with the first.

Chapter 4

12:24

Gina was eating a sandwich and reading when I came into the break room with my tacos from the food truck outside.

She looked up and put a finger on the page of her book, which was a Bible, I realized.

"How's it going?" she asked.

"You don't have to talk," I said. "I don't want to interrupt."

"I was just reading," she said.

It felt more like I'd walked in on her praying. Or at least warming up to it.

I gave it a beat, then sat down at the second table, so Gina could go back to reading if she wanted. But she folded a ribbon into the book to mark her place and closed it instead.

"Can I ask you a question?" she asked. My first thought was that it was going to be some kind of Jesus-y question, and I braced myself.

"Sure," I said.

"What's it like being Mark Schweitzer's kid?" she asked.

"Oh, wow," I said. "Big one in the first round."

She laughed and ate some sandwich.

"How much do you want to know?" I asked.

"Well, I think he's amazing," Gina said. "And he's obviously a genius. But he also basically lives at the lab. That's got to be hard."

"Not when you're two thousand miles away," I said. "You'd have to ask Violet about that. I haven't lived with Dad since I was fourteen."

"Was that part hard?" she asked. "When he left?"

I'd been feeling self-conscious about how I'd blown my whole nose story all over Gina and maybe gotten too personal on that first day, but I guess she could go there, too.

It wasn't a very interesting story anyway. Basically, Dad went to a conference in California one summer, met Felicia at a mixer, and started to "realize" that he'd never been in love with Mom. I'm not supposed to know that part, but oh well.

For a while, they'd tiptoed around the whole thing. Mom was unhappy. Dad was distant. Mom moved into Zoey's empty room. Dad went to California a lot. Then one day I came home from school and found two handwritten letters in sealed envelopes on the kitchen table.

I remember sitting on the edge of my bed with my coat still on, sweat dripping down my back while I read my letter. Eventually, I'd burn it in the bathroom sink, but not before I'd gone over it so many times that, even now, I could pull up most of what it had said. Something like

Dear Bear,

    I don't know how much of this speaks for itself and how much of it needs explaining. I also don't know what your mother will have told you by the time she gives you this letter, but I trust her to be fair about it.

The thing was, Mom always came home after me on Mondays, Wednesdays, and Fridays, but Dad hadn't been around enough to know that.

I want you to know that you did nothing wrong here. This is nobody's fault,

Incorrect.

least of all, yours. Mom and I have agreed for quite a while that being together is not a good idea in the long run, even if we disagreed about how and when this split should happen.

Which I took to mean that he'd thought about waiting until David, Zoey, and I had all moved out, but then lost patience before I could get there.

In any case, it's done now,

As if by mysterious forces beyond his control

and I want you to know that I'm pulling for nothing but the best where you're concerned.

Which felt weirdly cordial, like the kind of thing a teacher might write in your yearbook.

I'm not going to condescend by asking if you want to come live with me instead of Mom. I know that's not what you want. You're probably pretty ticked off, which I understand. We'll talk soon, I promise,

Not if I had anything to say about it.

and you can ask me anything you want then.

Which turned out to mean exactly what it said. I could *ask* anything, and he'd decide whether or not to answer.

I know it may have been a shock to come home and find me gone like this. It wasn't a casual choice, but one that I hoped would spare you the most pain. That might be hard to understand right now, but you're young

And you're an asshole.

and I truly believe that it will make sense to you in time. Meanwhile, whether you can believe this or not, there is nothing more on my mind right now than your well-being. Nothing.

Emphasis on the nothing.

Love, Dad

I sometimes wonder if it would have been easier to know ahead of time that he was leaving, which is like weighing the advantages of losing someone to a car crash as compared to, say, watching them slowly wither up and die of cancer. Not that Mom and I were given the choice. Dad made sure of that. Whatever he thought was "for the best" always seemed to conveniently line up with what was easiest for him.

All of which was everything I didn't say to Gina while that last question of hers hung in the air between us.

Was that part hard, when he left?

"Not really," I said. "The weird part is when I see him on the news, or read about him in some random article. Not that it happens that often, but even I know he's a total genius."

"Is any of it interesting to you?" she asked.

It seemed like a complicated question.

"Some of it," I said. "Like the multiverse. Or quantum nonlocality. Things like that."

"Quantum what?" she asked.

I was surprised it hadn't stuck to her, working there at the lab. "It's about how two particles can interact over any theoretical distance," I said. "It's also called entanglement, and it kind of shuts down the whole idea of time and space as we know it. It's big stuff, in Dad's world."

"So I guess you haven't exactly been ignoring him, huh?"

"I guess that depends on if you mean Dad or his work," I said.

"Which is kind of my point," she said. "Sometimes I wonder if those things are one and the same."

I laughed.

"What?" she said.

"Nothing," I said. "Just . . . good call."

4:21

Dad came into the front office a little before four-thirty.

"Well, the good news is you don't have to ride with me to this first group meeting," he said.

"You're not coming?"

"I can't," Dad said. "I'll swing by to pick you up afterward, but I just can't get away that early."

I wanted to look over at Gina in the worst way. She'd basically called it in the break room just a few hours earlier. But she didn't need me putting a spotlight on that.

"Can I drive myself?" I asked. "Then I could come back and pick you up after."

"I tried Felicia," Dad said, "but she has staff supervision on Thursdays."

"So is that a no?" I asked.

"I could take him," Gina said.

I swiveled in my chair, and Dad looked at her.

"I'm sorry if I'm not supposed to know what we're talking about," she said, "but I wouldn't mind."

"Are you sure?" Dad asked. "Because honestly, I'm in a pinch."

"No you're not," I said. "See, I have this thing called a driver's license?"

Dad gave me a look.

"It's no problem," Gina said, and then looked at me half apologetically. "I mean, if you don't mind."

"He doesn't," Dad said, and I kept my mouth shut because basically I didn't. Gina was an unknown quantity, in terms of being stuck in a car together, but with Dad I knew exactly what I'd get, and not in a good way.

"You should be fine if you leave by ten after five," he said. "Thanks, G. I really appreciate it."

"Yepper," she said, and gave me another one of her winks. I think it was supposed to acknowledge the inside joke we suddenly had. Or the inside something, anyway.

5:35

"What time's your meeting?" Gina asked.

"Six o'clock," I said. "I'm supposed to be there at quarter of, but you can take your time."

"We've got this," she said, and sped up to make it through a yellow light.

It turned out that Gina drove a whole lot like Wexler.

Which is to say, not the way I expected someone like her to drive. Maybe for her, a fatal car crash was more of a pro-con situation than a solid problem, since the consolation prize was a literal eternity in heaven.

"Let me ask you something," I said. "If it's okay."

"You can *ask* me anything," she said.

"Well, you're a, um—" I wasn't sure if "born-again Christian" was correct, or maybe offensive. "My dad said you're a born-again Christian," I said.

"Yeah?" she said.

"Is that okay to ask?" I asked her.

"It's fine," she said.

I'd never been to a Sunday church service in my life, which is a kind of shorthand for how little I knew about Gina's world. The closest I ever came to thinking about Jesus was when I flipped past those preachy shows on TV. Or once in a while, I'd see a crucifix and wonder what it was like to have spikes driven through your hands and feet. But that was about it. I still didn't get why some people felt the need to download their beliefs from some mythical place on high, but I also didn't pretend to understand any of it. Or care, really. It was Gina I was curious about, not Jesus. So I kept going.

"I guess I just wondered why you'd work there," I said.

"At the university?"

"In physics," I said. "Isn't a lot of that against what you believe? Like the big bang and whatever?"

She bunched her lips, which had a fresh coat of ballpoint red on them. I wondered if she ever changed shades, or if it was always the same look, like a cartoon character, or a superhero.

"Well, I *was* transferred over when they eliminated the study abroad program, so it wasn't my choice," she said. "But I like it. You don't have to be an atheist to admire scientific genius."

That was fair enough. "Do you believe in evolution?" I asked.

She took a breath—impatience, frustration maybe. "Let's say science and I have our disagreements, but they're not chronic."

"Disagreements with science?" I said. "That's like disagreeing with facts."

"Whose facts?" she said.

I didn't even understand the question.

"Whose facts are you talking about?" she tried again. "Whose science?"

"Everyone's," I said. "Anyone's. It doesn't belong to someone. It just is."

"See, that's how I feel about God," she said, then signaled a left turn and sped up to make it ahead of a truck turning the other way. "I mean, who's to say that He doesn't have a hand in the way particles behave, or carbon dating, or whatnot?"

"He, God?" I asked. The other possibility, albeit a vague one, was that she meant Dad.

"Yes, God," she said. "Just because people figure this stuff out doesn't mean He didn't get there first."

"Why would he?" I asked.

"Why anything?" she said. "We don't get to know the answer to that, and that's true whether you believe Jesus Christ is your savior or not."

I was starting to get uncomfortable. It didn't feel like she was trying to convert me exactly, unless, of course, the conversion was designed to not feel that way for strategic reasons, in which case, I was totally falling for it.

But at the same time, I couldn't help noticing that by default, the closest thing I had to a friend in California was—

"How old are you, anyway?" I asked.

"Twenty-eight," she said. "Why?"

"Just curious."

—a twenty-eight-year-old born-again Christian secretary with a red-lipstick habit and an apparent jones for speed.

Duly noted.

5:45

I didn't get nervous until the front door of Linton Family Services swung closed behind me. Then it was like everything reset. My mind went blank, and, just as fast, started filling up with all kinds of not knowing what I was supposed to do.

"Can I help you?" a woman behind a desk asked.

"Yeah, I'm here for, um . . ." What was I there for? "Martina Williams's thing?"

"Sure," she said, and pointed me down the hall, where Martina was waiting in the only open doorway.

"Hey, Chris. Glad you made it," she said. "Have a seat anywhere."

The room was huge, with a circle of chairs at one end, mostly filled by the other guys. My heart was beating faster just thinking about trying not to look as nervous as I felt. Or as hickish. Apparently all of the drug offenders in California were cooler-looking than I was. I'd never spent much time being *from* Ohio before. It had mostly been eighteen years of being *in* Ohio. Until now.

"Phones off, please and thank you," Martina said, taking the last chair in the circle. "Hi, everyone. As you can see, we have a new member tonight. This is Chris."

I raised my hand just high enough (no pun intended). "Hey," I said.

"Let's go around and introduce ourselves by name," Martina said, and looked at the kid on her right to start.

"What's up, Chris, I'm Brendan," he said. He was on the younger end, like me, in a loosened tie and a short-sleeved shirt.

"Trent," said the next guy. Hoodie up, dirty plaid shorts.

"Bill." Insurance. I bet he sold insurance.

"Hey, man, I'm Danny." The oldest guy by far, with two full-sleeve tattoos, including black dots on the tips of all his fingers.

"Biz." The opposite of Danny. He looked about thirteen, even though the group was eighteen and over. He had a longboard, deck down, under his chair.

"Hey. My name's Tucker. I'm glad you made it in, man." Obese. Crazy hair. Yellow glasses. "It's never easy at the beginning, but I guess that's what they say, right? It is what it is. I know for me—"

"We're just going to start with names, Tucker," Martina said, and looked at the next guy.

"Hey, I'm Salvatore." Wedding ring. Football ring. Tie tack. Gold chain. Sad eyes.

"Pete." Tank top, muscles, more tattoos, and a beer belly.

"Swift. Hi, Chris."

"Did you say Swift?" I asked.

He was definitely the best-looking one in the group. Dark eyes, nice arms, cool glasses. And lots of thoughts I probably wasn't supposed to be having. Like whether or not he worked out. And if he was into guys.

"Swift," he said again.

"I'm Burton," the next guy said. College student, I was guessing. Huge ratty backpack on the floor.

"Hey, I'm Ken." Pale, soft, unthreatening. Programmer, maybe. Gamer, maybe. Both, maybe.

"Okay, thanks, everyone," Martina said. "Moving on."

But I was still back on Swift, wondering what kind of underwear he had on. And about where his name came from. Jonathan Swift. That was the *Gulliver's Travels* guy, right?

"We're going to start with a simple focusing exercise," Martina said.

The room was hot, but the AC had just kicked on, blowing cool air and white noise down on us. Swift was sweating. So was I. And Martina was still talking.

". . . in through your nose, and out through your nose, all at your own pace," she said slowly, with her voice at about half volume. "Notice any thoughts you're having, and then just let them float on through."

Everyone else had their eyes closed. Martina gave me an encouraging smile and kept going.

"There's nowhere you have to be right now. Nothing you need to be doing. Just notice your breath. In. And out. All at your own pace . . ."

I closed my eyes.

I breathed in through my nose, and out through my nose.

In through my nose, out through my nose.

"Notice your body. Feel your feet against the floor, your back against the chair. . . ."

In through my nose, out through my nose.

In, out.

Dad.

He popped into my head out of nowhere.

Then Anna.

Then Wexler.

Replaced by Swift. I half opened my eyes. He had his shoes off and his hands were on his knees. His eyes were still closed.

I closed mine again.

In through the nose, out through the nose.

"This isn't about thinking more clearly. It's about *experiencing* more clearly. All you have to do is notice whatever it is you're noticing—about this room, this moment. . . ."

As it went on, I caught little glimpses of what I think Martina was going for. I'd breathe for a few seconds, and everything would float away, but it never lasted long. My head kept crowding up all over again.

"And now bring your attention back into the room," she finally said. "Take three more easy breaths, and when you're ready, go ahead and open your eyes."

When I did, I forced myself to look at Martina, not Swift. I didn't want to get caught staring, even though I definitely wanted to stare.

From there, everyone went around and did a check-in. Most of them talked about how their week had gone, and whether they wanted to use, or drink, or if they had a fight with their girlfriend, or whatever else. The big guy, Tucker, talked way more than anyone else. I felt sorry for him, like this might be the only place where people ever listened to what he had to say.

I felt sorry for myself, too. I missed Wexler. I missed Anna. I missed knowing that these next two months were going to play out the way I wanted them to. It was supposed to be the best summer I'd ever had, this once-in-a-lifetime bridge between high school and college.

But now, instead, somehow—this.

Except, not *somehow*. I knew exactly how.

Despite what Dad might have thought, I knew this whole situation was a shit cake of my own making. Dad was just in charge of the frosting. Which wasn't to say he had to pile on so much of it. But still, I was the one who had screwed up—accidentally, yes, but undeniably—and the more it settled over me, the more I hated myself for it.

Even so, I was shocked when I felt the tears start to sting

my eyes. It was like an ambush, and by the time I realized it was happening, there was nothing I could do to stop them. I just put my head down and hoped nobody would notice.

The problem being that we were all in a circle.

I didn't like to imagine what the others might be thinking, but there was nothing I could do about that, either. I was stuck here, in more ways than one. So I squeezed my eyes shut like they were taps I could turn off. I bore down with my whole body, willing my throat to cut off the sob that wanted to come out. I gritted my teeth and curled my toes and waited for all of it—any of it—to pass.

Chapter Four

11:10

Wexler got cut early, but he waited for me to finish my shift so we could head out together. Anna was waiting for us to come find her, either at the Bean or walking around downtown. She wouldn't be hard to find.

"What do you want to do tonight?" Wexler asked me.

"Do you want to just drop me off at home?" I asked.

"What do you mean?" he said. "I just waited for you."

He sounded kind of annoyed, even though I thought it was weird for him not to get where I was coming from.

That same old question, the one we asked ourselves all the time—*What do you want to do tonight?*—was a whole new thing now, fundamentally recolored by the fact that Wexler and Anna were officially going to want some time to themselves (= away from me), and probably on a regular basis. In terms of my last summer at home, it was like someone had rearranged the furniture and I was stuck trying to find my way around in the dark. What were the new rules? How long was I supposed to hang out?

"Don't be stupid," Wexler said, which I think meant he'd just figured out where I was coming from. "You want to go to a late movie?"

I did. "Let me see what's playing," I said, and pulled out my phone while I sent a little wave of gratitude his way.

The truth is, I was about half in love with Wexler. Which is to say, I didn't want to do him any more than I'd want to do my own brother, but I could easily see how he'd managed to get some kind of naked with some two-digit number of girls since freshman year.

My own number was something very much like zero, assuming that making out in the bathroom with Andy Goldreyer's cousin at a cast party for *Brigadoon* junior year didn't count. So far, my entire sex life was a one man, one hand kind of deal, and it was looking pathetically possible that I was going to start college with the same stats.

"There she is," Wexler said, pulling over outside the Bean. Berylin was there, along with some cluster of other people I couldn't make out in the dark.

"Anna, your husbands are here," Berylin said when we pulled up.

"Hi, honeys, did you have a nice day at work?" Anna said, coming over. She got into the front seat while I moved to the back.

Berylin came over, too, and leaned in the window. "What are you guys doing tonight?"

"Movie," Wexler said.

"Can I come? What are you seeing?" she asked.

"Actually," Anna said. "I just need to talk to these guys. Sorry, sweetie."

"Omigod, you three really need to move to Utah," she said. "It's totally nauseating, you know that, right?"

"Completely," Anna said, and squeezed Berylin's hand before Wexler pulled away from the curb and ripped them apart.

And then we were out.

There was only one theater with midnight movies, so we got onto Jameson Pike and headed out of town. We'd figure out what to see on the way.

Then, before we'd even passed the THANKS FOR VISITING GREEN RIVER, A GREAT PLACE TO LIVE! sign, Anna turned around to look at me.

"Do we need to talk about what happened?" she asked.

"I don't know," I said. "Do we?"

"I just don't want it to be awkward," she said.

"Me neither," I said.

"So let's make a pact," Anna said.

"Pact?" Wexler said. "That sounds kind of suicidey."

"Call it whatever you want," she said. "But I want both of you to promise me you'll say something if it gets weird, and I'll do the same. Okay?"

"Sure," Wexler said. I figured that was a maybe.

Anna looked right at me again. "How are you doing?" she asked.

"It was weird for about five minutes," I said. "But I'm fine."

"I don't want you to feel bad," Anna said.

"I'm fine," I said. It was a half lie. I felt half bad.

"All right," she said. "Let me ask you this then. Am I the only one who thinks it's kind of conspicuous that we're in the front and you're in the back—and I mean like in a way we wouldn't have even thought about twenty-four hours ago?"

Neither of us gave an answer, but Anna wasn't waiting for one. She just twisted around in her seat, climbed up and over, and landed in the back next to me.

"Yeah, this isn't any weirder," I said. But mostly I was thinking, *I love my friends. So much.*

"Right?" Anna said, and put her head on my shoulder. "Because nothing has changed."

"Except the parts that have," I said.

"Right," she said. "Except for that."

11:20

So that was it. I'd had my chance to say something. Now it was gone. Not that I couldn't bring it up again later, but I knew I wasn't going to. I mean, was there any version of that conversation where I didn't look like a selfish whiner who couldn't just be happy for his friends?

Probably not, considering all the thoughts running through my head just then.

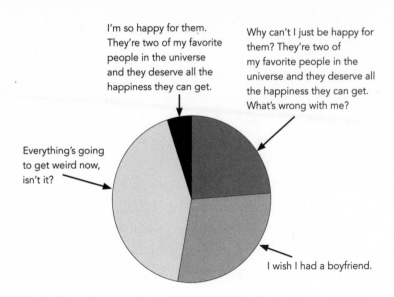

I'm so happy for them. They're two of my favorite people in the universe and they deserve all the happiness they can get.

Why can't I just be happy for them? They're two of my favorite people in the universe and they deserve all the happiness they can get. What's wrong with me?

Everything's going to get weird now, isn't it?

I wish I had a boyfriend.

Either way, the brute fact was this: My probability of finding someone in Green River was exponentially lower than Wex's or Anna's. It just was. They had hetero math on their side.

Which isn't to say that I wasn't thinking about other guys all the time. I mean, let's be honest, horny's a full-time job. But I also wasn't fooling myself that after eighteen years in the same small town, some new possibility was going to crop up out of nowhere.

Just one more reason I couldn't wait to get to Birch in the fall.

Still, none of that seemed worth saying out loud. So I sat there, staring straight ahead. The road was just a tongue of light gray in Wexler's headlights, and I watched the passing lines go by like an endless series of Morse dashes, until my thoughts landed somewhere else. Somewhere safer, and more comfortable.

I turned on my camera first. Then I pointed it at Anna, catching her face, on and off, in the headlights of the cars going by.

"Do you ever feel like there's something more going on out there?" I asked.

"How do you mean?" she asked.

"I mean, say there are all these infinite parallel universes, and I'm in some of them, or all of them. Who's to say I don't experience all those possibilities on some level?" I asked.

"Hm," Anna said. "Like touching infinity."

"Exactly," I said. "I like that. Touching infinity."

"Sounds like a band name," Wexler said.

"And what about time?" Anna asked. "Now that you mention it."

"What about it?" I asked.

"I mean, is it *now* in all of those possibilities? Wednesday at 11:20 in infinite different ways? Or is it literally all different times, all the time?"

"Good question," I said. "Maybe 'now' is all we can see because our little unevolved brains think that's all there is, like the way a goldfish thinks he lives in a bowl-sized universe."

"Did you just make that up?" Anna asked. She turned on the seat to face me.

"The words, not the idea."

"Oh, right. Of course. What does your dad say about all that?"

"I don't know," I said, and turned off the camera. I didn't want to talk about Dad, but Anna saw right through me.

"Stop already," she said, and grabbed my hand in the dark. "Okay? He left four years ago. Let's pry that cold icicle of resentment out of your little baby fist once and for all."

"Dang," I said. "I'm hurt."

"Except you're not," she said.

"I know," I said. "I'm not, but—"

But I could have been. That's what she didn't seem to see.

"Why do you hate him so much?" Anna asked.

I still wasn't interested in this subject, but I tried to give her a real answer anyway.

"Because of what he did to Mom. And me. And because of how he did it. Also, because he's this huge, legitimately important brain who thinks *that* gives him some kind of pass for also being a generally shitty person."

"In that order?" Anna asked. It was the perfect question, and made me smile. For a second, anyway.

"God, how am I going to get out of this wedding?" I asked.

"I don't think you are," Anna said. "But, I mean, do you think you even should? It *is* his wedding, after all. Not some regular summer vacation thing."

"I know," I said. I knew, I knew. It's not like I thought I

wasn't being an asshole about the whole thing. Zoey had already made that perfectly clear. It was more like I couldn't bring myself to care. What I really needed was the nerve to tell Dad I wasn't going to be there.

"Hey, it could be worse," Wexler said. He caught my eye in the rearview mirror. "If your mom and dad knew what really happened to your face? Could be a lot worse."

He was right about that. Wexler's specialty was silver linings.

"Yeah, right?" I said. "Especially Dad. He'd probably make me come out there for the whole summer, working at his lab so he could keep an eye on me, or whatever."

The idea of it made my skin crawl. I shivered it off. "God, can you imagine?" I said.

"Isn't that the point?" Anna asked.

"Huh?"

"I mean, *can* you imagine? Because if everything exists, then doesn't that mean you *are* out there and all of that *is* happening?"

"Good point," I said. "Which of course raises the other question: Is it happening because we're imagining it, or are we imagining it because it's happening?"

"Okay, my head just exploded," Wexler said.

"Well, don't stop driving," Anna said. "I don't want to miss the previews."

I leaned up to look at the clock on Wexler's dash. The movie didn't start until midnight, and it was only 11:22.

"We'll be fine," I said.

2:41

When I got home that night, I had an email from Birch on my laptop, with the name of my roommate for September

Neerav Seles. New York, NY

and a link if I wanted to message him.

I stared at his name for a long time. My acceptance letter in March had been the first cracking open of that door, the first time I actually *felt* like I was going away to college. Now another crack was letting in a little more light. Instead of Theoretical Roommate, I had Neerav Seles, NYC.

This was the guy who'd come back from an exam and I'd say, *How'd it go?* And he'd say, *Sucked.* And I'd say, *I think they're serving pizza tonight.* And he'd say, *Let's eat.*

Or maybe we'd have a huge, somehow controversial fight in the first month and one of us was going to have to move out.

Or he was going to get hit by a falling satellite a week before he was supposed to start college, and we'd never meet after all.

But for sure, something something something, Neerav Seles, NYC.

Detail by detail, the next part of my life was filling itself in, and the bigger that picture got, the smaller Green River felt. Or maybe the town was exactly the same, but I just didn't fit there anymore.

After eighteen years of living around the same four thousand people, walking up and down the same streets, and doing the same five or six things there were to do, I felt like I was drowning in sameness. And the only things that had changed were things I wished would go back to the way they'd been. Because now, with the whole Wex and Anna situation, it seemed like there was just a little less room for me where I was—and a little more reason to go.

The best I could do in the meantime was keep focusing on that other picture, the one I couldn't wait to step into. So I sent Neerav a quick note to make it all just one detail closer to real.

> Hi Neerav. It looks like I'm your roommate in Bremen Hall this fall. I don't really know what we're supposed to cover at this point, but I just wanted to say hello. Let me know if you want to talk sometime.
>   Chris Schweitzer

1:18

Mom took me shopping for a blazer the next day. I didn't need a tie for the wedding, but I didn't own a jacket or a suit. Which was maybe moot, seeing as how I was still hoping to get out of this whole thing, but I hadn't worked up the nerve to tell Mom that, much less Dad. I'd save the receipt, in any case. And in the meantime—

"He should be paying for this," I said, while Mom flipped through a bunch of options on a rack.

"Don't worry about it," she said.

I got mad when I thought about Dad taking advantage of her. She didn't want anything from him, except where Zoey, David, and I were concerned.

"Hey." Mom put a hand on my arm. She knew exactly what I was thinking. "You know, if you look closely, you'll see a little of the guy I married. And the guy who loves you, too. In the best way he knows how."

She held a blazer up against me and then handed it over on the hanger. "Try that on," she said, and kept looking.

"Okay, maybe he's doing his best," I said. "But doing your best doesn't mean you automatically get a good grade."

"True," Mom said.

"Maybe his best isn't good enough."

She didn't say anything to that. She never condescended to me by pretending Dad was someone he wasn't. She didn't condescend to me at all, which was maybe the biggest difference between the two of them. Every conversation with Dad felt like it was made of plastic in comparison.

She turned to hand me another jacket, but stopped to look at the one I'd just tried on. "That's not bad," she said.

I looked in the mirror. It was fine.

"How does it feel?" Mom asked.

It feels complicated, Mom.

"It's good," I said. I held out my arms to check the sleeves. "I can be done here if you can."

Mom reached over and looked at the price tag. "Sold," she said, and we headed for the register. Mom didn't love shopping any more than I did.

"Hey, by the way," she said, "what happened with the insurance interview at the restaurant?"

"Oh, that," I said. "They kept changing the time, but I'm supposed to meet with someone tomorrow."

I hadn't been talking about any of it with Mom, basically because it was easier that way. With everyone else, it felt like I was lying *at* them. With Mom, it felt like I was lying *to* her. As in, doing something to her that she didn't deserve.

"Don't I need to be there?" she asked.

"Actually, you don't," I said. "See, because eighteen years and two months ago, you went to the hospital and endured eleven hours of terrible pain to bring me into the world."

"That's my man," Mom said. It was an inside joke that had been running since my birthday, and it had kind of marked my entry into adulthood, that we could joke about it like that.

Then she tsked and took in a little shallow mom breath. I knew exactly what she was going to say. *How did you get to be eighteen?*

"How did you get to be eighteen?" she asked.

"Just lucky, I guess."

She put her arm around my shoulder and pulled me in, hard. Mom had three older brothers and she knew how to wrangle a person. "You're going to be amazing," she said.

"At what?" I asked.

I mean, besides lying to you.

"You choose," she said. "Whatever you want."

Chapter 5

7:07

As I sopped up the last of my chili with one of Felicia's amazing cheddar biscuits at dinner that night, I turned to Dad and asked him something I never would have even thought about a few weeks earlier. But now I was curious.

"Why didn't we go to church when I was little?"

Dad looked at me like I'd asked why we didn't go to Mars.

"Because your mother and I aren't religious people," he said.

"What do you believe in?" I asked. "Do you believe in God?"

"Have you really never talked about this?" Violet asked. I knew she'd had a bat mitzvah. David, Zoey, and I sent her a gift card. But she and Felicia didn't usually go to temple or anything like that.

Not to mention, there were a lot of things Dad and I had never really talked about.

"Since when are you religious?" he asked.

"I'm not," I said. He really didn't know me, did he? "I

was just curious. Gina and I were talking, and it got me wondering."

"You were talking to Gina about religion?" he asked, and his voice edged up a notch.

"Well, yeah," I said. "It's kind of a package deal."

"I talk to her all the time, and it never comes up," Dad said.

He also didn't sit next to her all day. Or try to know people outside of whatever role they served, relative to him. I'm pretty sure for Dad, Gina was a secretary who happened to be a person, not the other way around.

"The point is," Dad felt the need to add, "she's not exactly an unbiased source."

"Neither are you," Felicia told him from her side of the table. I was glad she said it instead of me.

"So you think it's all bullshit?" I asked Dad. "All religion?"

"I think its misused symbolism," he said. "But the symbols are quite rich. I understand the appeal."

"Isn't that what physics does? Creates symbols to represent the world as it really is?"

"Oh, please." Dad started folding his napkin. "Spare me the false equivalencies."

Violet looked up from her phone again, like some smaller animal on the veldt sensing conflict, unsure whether to hold still or flee.

"Mark, calm down," Felicia said.

"I am calm," Dad said. He seemed it actually, but I'll bet

she was thinking about that shattered glass from the first night. I know I was.

Then Dad turned back to me. "Please, just . . . don't find Jesus this summer," he said. "Okay? Not on top of everything else." Because apparently, I owed him one.

"What would be so wrong with that?" Felicia asked. "A lot of the happiest people I know are religious."

"And a lot of the unhappiest," Dad said. Then to me again, "Have you even asked her about the whole gay thing?"

"In fact, yeah," I said, even though I hadn't. "She's not as judgmental as you think."

"I didn't say she was judgmental."

"Sure you did."

"Don't start putting words in my mouth."

"Guys, come on . . . ," Felicia said. It was spiraling down, and I think the rest of her sentence was supposed to be something like *we were having such a nice dinner.* But now I was the one who wouldn't stop.

"Okay, not that I had any—like *any*—inclination to 'find Jesus,' whatever that means, but do you even hear yourself?" I asked. "It's always a lecture with you."

"Just because you don't like the conversation doesn't mean it's a lecture," Dad said.

Yeah, he definitely didn't hear himself. The whole exchange was a perfect reminder of why I'd spent as little time as possible interacting with Dad for the past four years. It never went anywhere worth being.

He wasn't done, either. "You're young," he said. "You're

impressionable. You hate your father. You think I don't see all that, but I do. It's not inconceivable that you could be, let's say, open to suggestion in a way that you might not have been under other circumstances."

The fact that he said *You hate your father* seemed to hang there, louder than anything else he'd just said. If I disagreed (enough) I might have corrected him.

"Okay, well, good talk," I said, and started to get up with my plate.

"Chris . . ." Felicia put her hand on top of mine. "Let's just change the subject."

"It's fine," I told her. "Violet, you want to help me clear, and then maybe play something?"

She perked up at that, like someone had just spoken English for the first time in a while.

"Sure," she said.

I'd been leaving Violet mostly alone, partly because of the creepy crush vibe she threw, and also because she was fourteen and not that interesting. But we did have this unexpected compatibility when it came to video games. It was something, anyway.

So we started clearing the table while I tried to reset and maybe not be an argumentative asshole for just a little while.

Maybe Dad could do the same.

10:05

When I opened my laptop later that night, I had a message waiting from Birch with the name and contact for my roommate that fall. The kid's name was Neerav Seles and he lived in New York City.

I still couldn't believe I'd actually gotten into Birch. And now I couldn't believe there was a chance it might not happen. I didn't fool myself for a second that Dad was bluffing about this whole arrangement, either. Trying to get out of a deal with my father is like trying to take back a fart.

So I printed out the email, stuck it in a drawer, and left it there, like some kind of souvenir from my possible future. I wasn't going to get too excited about Birch until I knew for sure I was going. And since I didn't feel like thinking about it anymore, I texted Wexler to see what he was up to.

What's going on back home?	

I was glad when he texted right back.

	Not much. Hanging.
Just you and Anna?	
	A bunch of people
Hi from me	

There was a long pause. Then I got a video of Anna, Berylin, Eddie, the Parkers, Lainie, Michaela, and Tyson, all hanging out at Eddie's.

"Okay, go," I heard Wexler, presumably from behind the camera.

"HI, CHRIS!" everyone yelled. Most of them drew out the words in a corny way, like Wexler was making them say it.

Anna and Berylin came in close then. Wexler swung up and over their heads and spun around, back onto Anna. She took the phone from him, kissed the lens, and pulled it back again.

"Hey," she said, in close-up. "You should be here, and I refuse to pretend that this doesn't suck, because it does. But we love you, and we miss you. Mmmmmwah!" Then Wexler leaned into frame and they both waved until she turned the camera off. That was it.

A second later, Wexler texted Anna and me.

Did you get that?		
	Yeah tx! Love it.	
		How's it going, sweetie?
	I've been better	
		I'm hugging you with three thousand mile arms
	You only need two	
		Arms?
	Two thousand miles	
		It feels like more

	It does	
I thought we were supposed to be cheering him up		
	You are	
		We are
If you say so		

They were, kind of. But that video also showed me exactly what I was missing, including the fact that I was the only one missing it. I'd known most of those people since fourth grade or earlier. Lainie and I were born three days apart in the same hospital. The fact that I'd now been downgraded to a minor character in everyone's last summer together was suddenly gut-punching me with a whole new wave of disappointment. I would have killed to be there, even if it just meant sitting around and complaining about how there was never anything to do.

Now I couldn't stop thinking about how different everything would have been if I'd just stayed on my feet that night behind the restaurant. Not passed out. Not set down that whipped cream can at that exact moment. Not done whippets. Not gotten a job at Smiley's to begin with.

Not a lot of things.

11:55

It wasn't until later, lying in bed and watching that video again that I noticed the way Wexler leaned into Anna at the very end. There was something about how he pressed the side of his face against hers. It drew a line in my mind, right back to that question I'd asked Wex in the car on our last morning together.

Are you going to fuck Anna?

No, he'd said. Twice. *No.* But we all know what a negative plus a negative makes. So now they were. I was as sure of it as I could be without knowing it for a fact.

I wondered if it would have been the same if I'd stayed home. I didn't want to flatter myself, but maybe I was like that plastic strip they put in battery packs to keep the contacts from rubbing up against each other until you want them to. And now, with that plastic strip (= me) two thousand miles away, they were free to rub up against each other all they liked.

Which was fine. On paper.

It was even a good thing. In theory.

Wexler and Anna were the best friends I'd ever had, and they deserved all the happiness they could get. It wasn't like I *wanted* to feel selfish and resentful about the whole thing. More like it just happened that way.

I also knew I wasn't going to ask them about it. What was the point of that? If they denied it, I wouldn't believe them. If one of them denied it and the other admitted it, that would be weird, too. And even if they both admitted it . . .*

ARE YOU GUYS SLEEPING TOGETHER?		
	Wexler says no.	Wexler says yes.
Anna says no.	They're both lying to me.	Anna is lying to me.
Anna says yes.	Wexler is lying to me.	*They're telling me the truth, but even that's not the answer I want. The answer I want is a different reality.

Chapter Five

3:14

The insurance adjuster apologized about six times for being late to our meeting. She'd texted twice on her way to Smiley's and showed up with a little girl who was at the counter now, eating a huge sundae while we talked in the back office.

"Can you tell me the last thing you remember?" she asked me.

The truth was that I remembered setting down the whipped cream can and nothing else until the ambulance came. But in this version of the story, that whipped cream can didn't exist.

In the version where it *did* exist, I lost my job and also had to deal with whatever prison sentence my father would put on me if he found out.

Yeah, no thank you very much.

"I was taking out a big bag of garbage and I didn't see the milk crate outside the door. All I really remember is stumbling over it," I said. "And then I remember the ambulance coming."

I wanted her to believe me, of course, but the fact that I was afraid she wouldn't was only making it harder to make sure that she did.

The good news was I'd already moved past the glowing, red-hot core of the lie itself. As soon as my nose hit that cement, the story was the same either way.

"Sorry?" I said.

"Excuse me?" she asked.

"I thought you just said something," I told her.

She shook her head, then kept going.

"What kind of shoes were you wearing?"

"These." I kicked my left foot out from under my chair.

"Can I see the bottom?" she asked, and took two pictures with her phone. "And who else saw you fall that you know of?"

"Nobody," I said. "But Wexler was the one who found me."

"Shawn Wexler?"

"Yes. Sorry. Shawn."

"And nobody else was in the restaurant?" she asked.

"No. Just us," I said. "We were on closing that night."

"Okay then," she said, sooner than I thought. She unclicked her pen, and it was like the sound of a key turning in a lock.

You're free to go.

"That's it?" I asked.

"I just need a signature," she said, and flipped her paperwork around toward me. "We have twenty-one business days from the date of your accident to honor the claim or file a dispute. And again, I'm sorry about taking so long to get out here."

I stopped with my own pen hovering over the signature line on the form.

"Dispute?"

She bunched her lips and shook her head to shorthand *It's unlikely*. "If any credible evidence comes up to refute your story," she said. "At that point, we'd have to examine the case to see if you'd subjected yourself to any civil or criminal penalties."

Civil penalties? *Criminal* penalties?

"But," she kept going, "assuming everything's in order, you probably won't even hear from us again. Just don't disappear to Mexico in the next two and a half weeks, okay?"

"That's funny," I said, "because I actually am going to Mexico."

"Seriously?"

"No, I'm kidding," I said. I think I entertained her, anyway. Not so much on purpose as by habit, especially when I'm nervous. I'd just done the emotional equivalent of lying to a lawyer, if not the legal equivalent, too. It was only when she chinned down at the form in front of me that I realized I hadn't even signed it yet.

"Oh," I said, and scribbled my name where it belonged. Or didn't belong, depending on how you looked at it. It was like walking deeper into the lie, through another door, and hearing that door get nailed shut behind me.

I was stuck in this version now. No turning back.

4:29

Mitch was on dish when I came out of that meeting. He was spraying down a flat of dirty plates with his back to me, and I didn't think he even knew I was walking by.

"So how'd *that* go?" he asked.

"Excuse me?" I said.

"Your little meeting," he said. "Shit's getting official. Are you in the clear?"

I didn't know what to say. I was already preloaded for paranoia with Mitch, after the last time. He wasn't intimidating, exactly, but he did have this thick outer wall of unknowability, which he may or may not have been trying to cultivate with me. It was like the more this went on, the less I knew, and the less I knew, the scarier he got.

So I made a snap decision to run right at it.

"Can I talk to you outside?" I asked.

He didn't look up. Instead, he opened the double-doored dishwasher and used a rack of dirty dishes to push a clean one out the other side. Then he closed it again and sent the machine back into beast mode, spitting and steaming like some kind of stainless-steel dragon. You could burn your hand on a fresh-washed plate in that place.

"Sure," he said finally, and I followed him out the back door.

As soon as we were outside, he pulled a pack of Camel Lights out from behind the big air-conditioning compressor. I waited for the restaurant door to slam shut before I started talking.

"Is there something you want to say to me?" I asked then. Straight up, because why not at that point? My heartbeat was thready. I hoped he didn't notice how nervous I was, but it was time to get some answers.

"No," he said.

"So then why—"

"You didn't trip on a milk crate, did you?" he asked.

My stomach dropped wide open at that, and echoed back with something that felt like *sheeeee-it*. I still wasn't sure if he was telling me or asking a question, and my answer pretty much depended on that information.

"Are you telling me or asking me?" I asked him.

He took his time lighting up. Then he pointed over at his car, parked next to the dumpster and three spaces away from mine. We were all supposed to park in back of the restaurant so customers could have the spaces near the entrance.

"Let's just say that if someone was sitting over there when you 'tripped' . . . ," he said, but then stopped again. His eyes flicked across the parking lot, and when I looked, I saw the insurance lady and her daughter, just getting into their minivan. She smiled and waved. I did the same, feeling like an idiot, and waited for them to pull away.

"I don't know what you think you saw, but you're wrong," I told Mitch. "I tripped and fell." It was starting to feel like a bumper sticker. I'd said it so many times, even I was going to start believing it.

"Then I guess you've got nothing to worry about," Mitch said.

"See, but the way you say that, it's like you're trying to give me something to worry about."

"I'm not," he said.

"Why are you messing with me?" I asked. "Do you want something?"

"No, no," he said. "Seriously. I'm just trying to tell you we're cool."

Which felt a whole lot like *We're cool*, followed by an unspoken *unless* . . .

Unless *what*, Mitch?

But I didn't ask because I didn't want to cut the wrong wire here. It still felt like I was one snip away from the big boom. And I couldn't thank Mitch for his discretion, either, because that was an admission I wasn't ready to offer up. At least not until I knew more.

"Well, good," I said instead, "because nothing happened."

Mitch nodded as he blew out a cloud of smoke, pocketed his lighter, dropped his butt on the cement, and stamped it out.

"Exactly," he said.

"So that's the immediate goal. Eighteen days until I'm off the hook with the insurance company."

"It shouldn't be a problem," Wexler said. "I haven't told anyone."

"I haven't, either," Anna said.

"Well, you know I haven't," I said.

"Then we're good," Wexler said.

"Unless," I said.

"Unless what?" Anna said.

"Well, more like unless *who*," I said. "I had a weird conversation with Mitch Mitchell today."

"Is that really his name?"

"I don't know," I said, answering Anna but way past being interested in that question.

I was lying flat on my back, on the engine-warm hood of Wexler's car, in a pull-off at the edge of a cornfield by the high school, looking up at the stars. Anna was on the hood next to me and Wexler was leaning against the driver's door. They didn't seem in any hurry to take off without me, which was nice for a change, but never a given anymore.

"I can't believe his parents named him that," Anna said. "Is his full name Mitchell Mitchell?"

"I bet it is," Wexler said.

"Anyway," I said. "He was probably sitting in his car in the parking lot at Smiley's when I had my accident."

"Probably?" Wexler asked.

I shrugged. "That's what he said. Or at least kind of said. He's being weird about it, in any case."

"What do you mean? Weird how?" Anna asked.

"Like, 'I know what happened, and I'm not going to say anything,' dot dot dot, 'unless.'"

"'Dot dot dot unless'?" Wexler asked.

"Like he wasn't threatening me but he wanted me to know he could," I said. "The point is, I think he's telling the truth, but I have no idea how much I need to worry."

"Who *needs* to worry?" Anna asked.

"You know what I mean," I said.

"Mitch is kind of baseline weird," Wexler explained, for Anna's benefit. She was the one who didn't work with him, or really know him other than who he was.

"And he was definitely working that night?" Anna asked.

"Yeah. I checked the schedule," I said. And then to Wexler, "That was the night we were seeing who could talk the fastest to customers without them noticing."

"Oh, right," Wexler said.

"I mean, not Mitch, but I remember him watching us do it, and he thought it was funny."

"Do you ever think maybe you're thinking too hard?" Anna asked me.

"I think it all the time," I said.

"I'd leave it alone for now," Wexler said. "Just don't do anything to piss him off, if you can help it. And, I don't know, maybe just keep your eyes open for something you might be able to do about it."

"*Do* about it?" I asked. "That's like the most nefarious thing you've ever said."

"Good word," Anna said. "I want to be nefarious."

Wexler shrugged in a you-never-know kind of way. "His mom's pretty weird, too. I'll bet she'd freak out if she knew what a pothead he is. I think he's stoned at work most of the time."

"What am I going to do, take pictures of him getting high?" I asked. "I don't really see that happening."

"I'm just saying, a little insurance couldn't hurt," Wexler said. "Then, if he makes a real move, you'll be ready for him."

It all felt kind of testosterone-y and escalation-heavy now. Wexler speaks that language, not me.

And then, out of the next, long silence, and once we were back to just staring up at the sky, Anna quietly said—

"Do you think his middle name is Mitchell?"

Something about the timing of it was explosively perfect. You could *feel* the funny, and we all burst out laughing, in that way that uses up all of the air in your lungs at once. The kind that hurts. I rolled off the car and fell onto the ground, just to do it, and Anna screamed—*screamed*—with laughter, like it was the only way to get more out.

And for a while anyway, the corn stood vigil, and the stars went into or out of alignment, whatever they were doing that night, and it was all lanes open ahead, just a straight shot down the highway of that summer, doing this, with them, being there, exactly where I'd want to be.

And whatever else happened, there would always be

that night, and every night we had left that summer, along with all the ones we'd already had that would always be.

Flow. That's what some people call it. Flow.

So I guess I was going to worry about Mitch some other time.

Chapter 6

5:05

"This is a little weird, I'm not going to lie," I said, sitting across a couple of pizza slices from Gina.

"What's weird?" she asked.

"This. You and me, getting pizza, on the way to my drug thing." I still didn't know what to call those meetings.

We'd left work early because we were both hungry and Dad said it was fine. Also because, to exactly nobody's surprise, Dad couldn't get away in time to take me. It was only the second time Gina had driven me, but it was already like a thing now.

"Weird?" she said again.

"Unpredictable," I said. "If someone had asked you a month ago to say what you'd be doing today, you never would have come up with this."

She shrugged. "As opposed to the other futures you can predict?"

Gina, it turned out, was kind of awesome, in an interspecies sort of way. Sitting at our desks, we were like two animals in the zoo, striking up a friendship from cage to cage, with no real threat of ever having to get along in the wild. And if I didn't understand all her caws, and she didn't get my grunts, it didn't really matter. At some point, the difference between us had become the entertainment.

"I don't need every little thing to be predictable," she went on. "I know God has a plan for me, and that's very comforting."

"My dad thinks it's all a kind of crutch," I said. "Like religion is an excuse for not thinking for yourself."

"Hm" was all Gina said. I think she was as impervious to Dad's opinion about all that as she was to mine. So I kept going.

"He also thinks that you think I'm going to hell," I told her. "I mean, you know I'm gay, right?"

She narrowed her eyes at me. "Oh, come on. Don't flatter yourself."

"What does that mean?" I asked. "Like I'm that lame? Or just that obvious?"

"You're not lame," she said, and sipped her Diet Coke and smiled.

"I'm not obvious."

"Would you care if you were?"

"No," I said. "I mean, mostly no. I guess."

"Then mostly fine," she said.

She had this weird way of controlling situations. I'm not even sure she knew she was doing it, but it was like Gina's life happened exactly on Gina's terms, which you might think was a given, until you realize how much of your own life isn't that way.

"Okay, then," I said. "Let me ask you this. *Do* you think I'm going to hell?"

That was really the one I'd been building up to, without quite knowing it.

Gina just shrugged. "I think you deserve as much happiness as anyone else on this planet," she said.

"Nice nonanswer," I said.

"Again, do you care?"

It was getting complicated. Gina was welcome to believe whatever she wanted, including (I'm guessing) that when the time came, people like me were headed straight to eternal damnation.

But still—*eternal.*

I mean, *did* I care if she thought I was going to hell? Not exactly. But by the same token, all it would take was for me to be wrong about this, given that one of us had to be, and then there I am in the afterlife thinking, *Well, shit.* Forever. Literally.

Because no matter what I believed, or didn't believe, it could never be anything more than the world's strongest *probably.* Nobody expects to start walking through walls anytime soon, for example, but on the level of quantum probability, that's only because it's never happened before.

Which means the good news is—anything's possible.

But the bad news is—anything's possible.

In the meantime, I wasn't ready to let Gina off the hook.

It was all so low stakes since we didn't know each other that well, and also weirdly fun to talk about, for the same reason.

"So what is it?" I asked. "Like a 'love the sinner, hate the sin' kind of thing for you?"

Gina took a breath. I couldn't tell if she was thinking about my question or calming herself down.

"Why do you think I have to hate anything to have my beliefs?" she asked.

"Because a lot of people like you hate people like me," I said.

"That's an ugly thing to say."

"Are you saying it's not true?"

Her lips pressed together and thinned. I didn't realize until just then that she was also stubborn.

"Listen," she said. "Nobody gets a pass from me for hateful behavior, or thoughts, for that matter. But they don't get to define Christianity for me, either, any more than you do. You're going to have to take my word for it that I want you to be happy. And I'm wanting that for you in the only way I know how."

It wasn't a completely satisfying answer. It was like she'd kept half the nutrition for herself, which was very Gina. Not greedy, just steadfast. And I definitely wasn't going to tell Dad about this conversation, either. It was too close to an affirmation of what he already thought, and too complicated to try to explain the rest.

The truth was, I liked Gina. I just wasn't sure I was supposed to.

"You're a hard woman, Gina Pascal," I said.

"I know you're kidding," she said.

"Mostly kidding, anyway," I said.

"I know that, too," she said. Then she raised her Diet Coke and tapped it against my Coke. "See that? We're getting to know each other better all the time."

6:18

That night's meeting started in all the same ways as the week before. We did the meditation thing, and then the check-in thing, all while I did the trying-not-to-get-caught-looking-at-Swift thing.

He smiled at me once. Then he noticed me looking a second time. And then I had to stop looking.

There was something literally attractive about him, like he lived on ground so steady, you couldn't help wanting to move in that direction. He was good-looking, and seemed smart, too, and funny, and confident, and kind of perfect, actually. Right down to the *kind of*.

So when it came time for someone to talk, I wasn't really paying attention. Not until I heard my name.

". . . Chris?" Martina asked.

"Excuse me?" I said, while everyone's (and Swift's) eyes pivoted onto me.

"You want to share a little about what brought you here?" she asked.

"Ohhh," I said, shifting gears. Trying to, anyway, but mostly feeling on the spot. "I don't really know what to say."

"Anything about your current situation would be fine. But if you don't want to go, that's okay, too. You can pass," she said.

I wanted to pass, but at the same time, that seemed kind of dickish. Everyone else had been pretty honest so far, and I felt like I owed them the same in return. Also, the silence while they waited for me to decide was suddenly more than I could absorb, so I just started talking.

"Well," I said, "I got to California a couple of weeks ago from Ohio. My dad made me come out here after, um . . ."

Already, my throat had constricted around the words, like they were too big and undigested to come up.

". . . I passed out doing whippets back home and broke my nose . . ."

On the upside, I realized, I wasn't going to have to say *whipped cream* at any point to get through this story.

". . . or didn't break it, depending on who you ask," I said.

I ran my finger over the new ridge of bone on the bridge of my nose, vaguely hoping it might be worth something here, like *cred*, if that was even a thing.

I'm not sure what I was expecting. It's not like anyone rolled their eyes or laughed, but they also didn't do anything at all. Most of them were looking at the wall by now, or at their laps, or some middle distance on the floor between us. I didn't know where Swift was looking, because I didn't have the nerve to check.

"So now I'm working at my father's lab for the summer, and coming to these meetings," I said. "And, um . . . that's it."

"His lab?" one of the guys asked.

"Like a meth lab?" someone said, and everyone cracked up.

"Physics," I said. "Over at UC."

"So you're here because of *whippets*?" another guy asked. I couldn't remember most of their names.

"I guess," I said. "I smoked a lot of weed in high school and drank some, too."

The truth was, I smoked some and drank a little, but I was padding my résumé out of blind desperation. It was getting pathetic.

"*Man . . .*" Danny flicked his hand at me, like turning an invisible page. "No offense, but why are you even here?"

"Hey, hey," Martina said.

"For real," Danny said. "It's a real question."

"My dad's making me come," I said. That got a couple of open glances around the circle, like they were pairing up to not take me seriously now.

"Do you even have a problem?" Trent asked. "Or did you just have an accident?"

I didn't understand the difference, and with everyone looking at me, I didn't have the mental bandwidth to figure it out.

"I don't know," I said.

"Listen," Martina said. "A problem is a problem, and when it's not addressed, it gets worse. Sometimes that's not about the substances, but about the way our choices impact our relationships with other people. Everyone's here for their own reasons. But you already knew that, didn't you, Trent?"

"Whatever," he said. Not in a mean way, exactly. More

like he knew me—or at least he'd known people like me before and didn't have respect for any of them. I should have just passed when Martina gave me the chance.

I also should have told Trent to shove his attitude up his ass. Not that I ever would. But I should have.

I guess I'd thought that even in my hickish, Ohioan, whippet-sucking lameness, I'd be a little special here. An oddity, or something. But instead, I just felt like a big nothing.

"All right," Martina said. "Let's refocus. I'd like to hear the rest of whatever else you have to say, Chris."

"I think that's all for me," I said. In fact, I had nothing more to say about it. Maybe ever.

And the end of that meeting couldn't come fast enough.

7:07

Afterward, I was standing on the sidewalk and checking my phone when I sensed someone looking at me.

I glanced up and Swift—*Swift*—was standing right there, like he'd come out of nowhere.

"Hey," he said.

"Hey," I said.

"Don't worry about those guys," he told me. "It's like if you weren't slamming heroin between your toes or waking up from a coma before you got here, you don't belong. It's bullshit."

"Which of those did you do?" I asked, half joking, before I realized it was a dumb thing to joke about.

Dumbass.

"Neither," he said. "Synthetics don't count in there any more than whippets. I'm like you."

That last part—*I'm like you*—registered in my gut, just above my stomach. It made me want to laugh, or more like giggle, which is why I held it down.

"So what are you doing now?" he asked.

"Nothing," I said. It seemed like the best way to leave the most options open. "Why?"

And in the micro moment before he spoke again, a shower of sparks shot through my mind, each one an indiscernible part of some larger universe of possibilities, in terms of what he might be about to say.

"You like shitty doughnuts?" he asked.

One of those sparks came rushing at me. It was a sun. It was *my* sun, already pulling me into its orbit. I could feel it, like a tug in my chest, daring me to take a step in his direction.

"Sure," I said.

"'Cause there's a place over on Claremont," he said. "I could give you a ride afterward, if you want."

And a cosmic bolt of lightning jump-started my little planet to life.

Everything with Swift was still completely undefined. But this (whatever it was) *had* just taken *a* step in *a* direction. That much I knew for sure. And he was definitely gay, I decided. Or realized. Or decided to realize.

But in the meantime, there was just one problem.

"My dad's coming to get me," I said.

My dad's coming to get me. Six of the biggest boner-killing words in the English language.

"Oh," Swift said.

"I mean, I could try calling him," I said.

I was already dialing.

"Don't worry about it. It was just an idea," Swift said, but then Dad was there, answering on speaker.

"I'm less than a minute away," he said.

"I was actually just going to say I could get a ride," I told him.

"From who?" Dad asked.

"One of the guys in my group," I said. "We were going to grab some doughnuts."

Dad didn't answer, and it took me a second to realize he'd already said he was coming, which in his world didn't bear repeating.

"But . . . I guess we'll have to do it another time," I said, looking at Swift. He shrug-nodded back.

"Be right there," Dad said, and we hung up.

"Sorry," I told Swift. "He's almost here."

"Yeah, that makes sense," he said. "Too bad. You would have really hated those doughnuts."

I laughed because it was funny, but also to cover how ridiculously disappointed I was. "I guess I'll never know," I said.

"Nah, we'll do it next week," he said, with a kind of confidence I couldn't even imagine. "You're coming back, right?"

Oh yes.

Yes.

Yes.

Definitely.

"Pretty sure," I said.

"Good," he said. And the way he looked at me, it was just a technicality that actual beams of light weren't coming out of his eyes and into mine.

When he chinned over my shoulder, I almost flinched. I'd thought he was about to touch me, and as soon as I realized he wasn't going to, I wished he had.

"I'm guessing this is you," he said. I could hear tires crunching to a stop at the curb behind me, and I hated the universe for its perfect (= terrible) timing. "Could I get your number?"

I gave it to him and he said he'd text his to me, because I had to go.

"So, I'll see you next week," I said.

"Yeah," he said. "You will."

Because apparently, around there, anything was possible.

7:08

"Who was that?" Dad asked, pulling away from the curb.

"Just a guy in my group," I said. I don't know what he thought the range of possible answers might be. "Swift."

"Swift? Is that his first name or his last name?" he asked.

"Good question," I said. I didn't actually know.

But it was easy to guess what Dad was thinking now,

anyway. He was wondering if something was up between me and Swift—which was basically the same thing I was wondering.

"I hope you're not thinking about dating, Chris," Dad said.

"Dating?" I said. That thought honestly never crossed my mind. Not *dating*.

"Is that even allowed?" Dad asked.

"There's no rule about it either way," I said, which was true. Martina had gone through all the basics with me before the first meeting. "But it doesn't matter anyway. He's not even gay. He said something about a girlfriend."

That last part came out like some kind of instinctive self-defense move. I knew it might have been a mistake as soon as I'd said it, but at the same time, this was the best thing that had happened to me since I came to California. I didn't want Dad anywhere near it.

We rode in silence for several blocks after that, and I sat there, replaying the whole Swift conversation in my head, and doing a little math on where I wanted this to go next. Which eventually brought me around to—

"Hey, so when exactly can I start driving, anyway? You never really said, and to be honest, there's no reason you need to chauffeur me around like this."

Dad stared straight ahead, thinking, I think.

"Tell you what," he said, and I got a little rush of hopefulness. "You finish these six sessions and if we're all good at that point, you can start using the car."

"Let's say three meetings," I said.

"No," Dad said. "All six."

"Four meetings," I said.

"Six."

"Five."

I was entertaining myself at that point, more than I was actually expecting any kind of bargain. Dad didn't even answer on the last one.

"Okay, fine," I said. "All six, but that's my final offer."

That got a smile. And maybe I should have stopped there, but I felt like I was on some kind of roll.

"You know, I bet Gina wouldn't mind driving both ways next time," I said.

He side-eyed me then, almost shyly, for Dad. "You really don't want to be alone in the car with me, do you?" he asked.

It was true, even if that wasn't the main idea right now. The idea was doughnuts with Swift, but it helped if Dad thought otherwise, so I went with it.

"What do you want me to say?" I asked. "Besides, if you're honest, you know you don't have time for all this back-and-forth away from the lab. Especially with the wedding coming up."

That was all true, too, which helped.

"I'll even promise not to find Jesus," I said, which got another smile, and then an actual laugh out of Dad.

"You know, it's funny," he said. "If your mom had any concerns about who you were hanging out with at home, she'd get a kick out of *this* being the issue."

"What concerns did Mom have?" I asked.

"Not born-again Christians, I'll tell you that much," Dad said.

"Wait. Are you talking about Wexler and Anna?" I asked.

And since when did Mom and Dad compare notes?

"It's nothing," he said, shutting it down with a wave of his hand. "Fine, fine. You can ask Gina about the driving tomorrow."

I was still wondering about what Mom might have said, or what Dad might have misunderstood, given his general incapacity for listening, but since I was coming out ahead, I let the rest of it go. I was already one big step closer to doughnuts with Swift. Now I just had to figure out the Gina part.

A second later, my phone dinged. I looked down and saw a text from a number I didn't recognize.

	This is me. See you next week!

My mind fizzed like a fresh-poured Coke as I texted back.

Thanks, Me. See you then!	

Dad glanced over. "One of your friends from home?" he asked.

"Yeah," I said. "Wexler. He's just saying hi."

"Well, it's nice to see you smiling," Dad said.

In fact, I think I might have smiled all the way home.

Chapter Six

1:24

I hoped Dad wasn't going to be able to talk for long when I called. I wasn't looking forward to this conversation. Nothing new there except for the degree of dread. I just wanted to be over and done with it. Him. Both.

"Good afternoon," he answered, like he'd been waiting for my call.

"Sorry I didn't get back to you sooner," I said. "I just really wanted to think this through."

"Go on," he said.

"Well, I thought about it a lot," I said, "and I'm not sure it makes sense for me to be at the wedding anymore."

No answer.

"You can talk to Mom if you want," I said, "but it's my decision, and I don't think I'm coming."

There was another long pause. Dad always kept people waiting while he thought. Zoey, David, and I called it idling, as in, *Dad just sat there idling at the other end of the line while I waited for him to say something.*

"Okay," he finally said. "I've been thinking about it, too, and let me lay this out for you from my perspective."

No answer. Because I can play that game as well as he can.

"Are you listening?" he said.

"Go on," I told him.

"I'm chipping in sixty thousand dollars a year, starting in September, for you to go to Birch."

"Whoa, whoa, whoa. Where is this headed?" I asked, even though it seemed pretty clear.

"Don't you think there might be some tension between you not coming to my wedding and me supporting you through an expensive education?"

He was right, of course, especially if he only looked at his side of the picture, which was classic Dad. He never seemed to get that I might not be particularly interested in his Whole New Life—the one that walking out on us seemed to have afforded him.

"Dad—"

"You can get a great education at a state school," he said. "I went to a state school."

"Dad—"

"You only get to go to the more expensive school because we have a relationship. Take away that condition—"

That condition.

"—and it changes everything. Obviously, it's your choice to come out here or not, but choices don't happen in a vacuum."

"So, if I don't come to your wedding, you're not paying

for Birch," I said. I could almost always take my father's fifty words and turn them into ten. "Is that it?"

"Do you think that's unfair?" he asked back.

I think you walking out was unfair.

I think you changing the rules at this moment is unfair.

I think you holding your money over me is unfair.

I think that fucking letter was unfair.

I think that letter was the definition of unfair. You figured you could walk out on us with or without a big face-to-face confrontation, and in your world that's easy math. So you wrote a letter. You mitigated the damage (to you). And you let me hate you from a distance, because, in the mistake-free sterility of your world, that's what passes for a nonviolent choice.

"Yeah. Kind of," I said.

"*Kind of?*" he asked. "Can't you commit to anything?"

My father's not a *kind of* kind of guy, and every reason I'd been glad for not living with him over the last four years was going off like fireworks in my head.

"I didn't say I'm not coming. I just said I'm not sure—"

"No," he said. "That's not what you said."

"I'm going to try to come—" I tried again. I was doing C-minus work at this, at best. It was getting embarrassing. Not that it mattered anymore, because two things were obvious by now.

One, I was going to that wedding. If Dad said he was putting Birch on the table, I had no doubt that he meant it. It wasn't even worth talking about anymore.

And two, my father was never going to change. I don't know why that seemed like new information all of a sudden, but there it was. Maybe it was something I had to learn multiple times before I really got it.

Dad was Dad.

Dad would always be Dad.

Dad was constitutionally incapable of being anyone but Dad, which is to say, he was never going to be the father I wanted him to be.

Never.

And the only thing that didn't suck about that was that now I knew.

11:20

"How'd it go?" Wexler asked, when I got to the platform that night. He and Anna were already hanging out, and it was too hot, and way too humid to do anything else. I'd been sweating since I got out of the shower after work.

"Kind of like, *'I'm not coming'* and *'The hell you're not,'*" I said.

"He said that?" Anna asked.

"Basically," I said. "I go to the wedding or he's not paying for Birch."

"Wow," Wexler said. "No offense, but your dad's an asshole."

"No offense taken," I said. It was more like the opposite: defense appreciated.

Anna didn't say anything at all, which maybe meant she thought I was the asshole for even trying to get out of this. But she wasn't going to call me on it. She was too good a friend for that.

"So basically, I go to that wedding or change to a state school," I said.

"Oh! You know what?" Wexler sat up. "You could go to OSU! We could totally room together!" He put his hand up for me to confirm it.

Anna gave me a quick look. She knew what I was thinking. I loved Wexler, no exceptions, but the idea of staying in Ohio and rooming with him in September was like the opposite of where I wanted my life to go next.

Still, try saying that out loud.

"If it comes down to it, I'm all over that," I said. "But I pretty much have to go now. The only question is how little time I can get away with being in California."

"Well, at least you're not that other version of yourself," Wexler said. "The one who had to go out there and live with your dad all summer. His life sucks way worse than yours."

I was a little surprised. That wasn't a game Wexler usually liked to play. It was more of a Chris and Anna thing, but I liked when he did it.

"Although, who knows?" Anna said. "Maybe going out there would mean you'd meet someone you never would have met."

"Like a boyfriend?" I asked.

"Not necessarily," Anna said. "But the fact that you asked makes me think maybe that's what it should be."

"Are you saying I'd have to go to California to find someone who's into me?" I asked, just playing around— but playing with what might be true.

"Why not?" Anna asked. "Maybe going to California is exactly what it takes. And he's the best thing that ever happened to you, and hot, of course, and completely out of your league—"

"Um, thanks?"

"Except he's *not*," she said. "That's the thing. You just *think* he is, because you always underestimate yourself. See, you have no idea he's even noticing you until he starts talking to you out of the blue one day. And then maybe he kisses you in some doughnut shop somewhere, and everything changes."

"Why doughnuts?" I asked.

Anna just shrugged, but I knew. Randomness didn't need an explanation between us.

It was fun to think about anyway, like sending a care package to another version of myself. If he had to be stuck out there all summer with Dad, it seemed like a boyfriend was the least we could do for him.

I just hoped that he—Chris—I—appreciated it.

"Yeah, okay," I said. "I like this. What's his name?"

She thought about it. "Maybe something literary," she said. "Like Dickens."

"That sounds like a porn name," Wexler said.

"Good point," she said. "Longfellow then?" And we all cracked up.

It got quiet after that. I was still trying to think of a good name when Wexler spoke up next.

"All right, well . . . ," he said.

That was it, just those three words, but I could tell right away what they meant. He and Anna were about to take off. Alone.

This was a first. I was being dismissed for the night. They'd never had that power over me, and now that they did, I had no say in it at all. The change was as sudden as it was complete.

"I think we're going to take off," Wexler said, finishing the thought. If I wasn't mistaken, it was weird for him, too.

"Yeah. Sure," I said. I sat up and dropped off the platform to put my feet on the grass. I'd been thinking about what kind of video we might shoot that night for my (our? my?) Untitled Wex-Anna Project, but that obviously wasn't going to happen anymore.

"Do you mind?" he asked.

Did I mind? Of course I did. But did I object?

"Of course not," I said.

My car was parked next to his in the cul-de-sac at the edge of the golf course. It wasn't like I was going to stay out there alone, so we all walked back together.

"I'll talk to you guys later," I said when we got there.

"Good luck with your dad," Wexler said.

"Have a good night, sweetie. Sleep tight," Anna said, and they got into his car while I got into mine.

I sat there for a minute, watching them take off. I was thinking maybe I'd just call Dad right there and get it over with.

Then my phone dinged, with a text from Anna.

	What about Swift?

I couldn't help smiling. I mean, yeah, this sucked (for me), but I didn't need to overthink it, either. Anna was still there. Wex was still there. Not everything had changed.

And apparently now some version of me had a boy-friend named Swift. Why not?

Swift. I like it.	
	Me too. xo
xo	

11:50

I waited until I got home, then called Dad right away. There was no thinking I could put this off. No reason to anymore, either.

"I just wanted to let you know I'm coming, Thursday to Sunday," I told him. That would put me in California for the same number of days as David and Zoey, which meant I wouldn't have to be too alone with Dad. It was also the same Thursday that the insurance deadline ran out at the restaurant, so hopefully by the time I got back from the wedding, I'd be home free for the rest of the summer, on all counts.

Knock wood.

"Okay" was all Dad said. Friendly. Ish. He didn't ask about the flight times or question the short trip, which was unlike him. I asked if they were registered anywhere, and he said I shouldn't bother getting them a gift. For once, we were both tiptoeing around each other. It was awkward but unemotional, like two robots trying to play a real father and son.

There was a long silence then, and I realized I was waiting for him to say something, and he was probably waiting for me, since he'd spoken last. It went on just long enough to feel like a standoff, and another second later, I caved.

"So, I'll talk to you later?"

"Sure," Dad said.

"Okay. Well, bye."

"Have a good night, Chris."

"Good night."

I hung up and took a deep breath. Then another. Every time I got off the phone with Dad, it was like I'd eaten too much of something. It left me with this stuffed feeling in my head, and I just wanted to let my brain open up its pants and flop out on a couch somewhere to digest for a while.

But it was done. I was going. And it was fine. Whatever.

11:38

We had brunch at my house the next day. I texted Wex and Anna in the morning, and they came over.

Mom's not much of a cook but she made french toast. I made fruit salad. Wex and Anna brought coffee and fresh OJ. I took some more video and got them talking about their favorite memories from high school. It was nice. Again.

"Thanks, Beth," I said as Mom put seconds onto my plate.

"Anna? A little more?" Mom asked.

"No thanks. I'm stuffed," Anna said.

"Wex'll have hers," I said. Wex wouldn't have asked for himself, but he ate more than anyone I knew. It was stunning, sometimes.

Mom slid some french toast onto Wex's french toast and started another batch.

"So, how long have you two been a thing?" she asked, without looking over.

Wexler grinned. Anna's jaw dropped. She looked at me and mouthed, *You told her?*

I didn't know she knew, I mouthed back.

What? Anna asked.

Never mind, I answered. It was too complicated for mime.

"What makes you think we are?" Anna asked. Her tone made it clear she wasn't denying anything. More like investigating the leak.

Mom turned to look at us. "Listen, guys, just so you know, if *this*"—she wagged her spatula at Wex and Anna—"is supposed to be a secret, you're going to have to do a little better."

"Um, thanks for the tip?" Anna said.

"I'm just saying," Mom went on. "All those adults you navigate around all the time? They're not virgins."

"Okay, okay, nice chat," I said.

"You see that?" Mom said. "He'll talk to me about anything *but* sex."

Wexler laughed.

"What?" I asked.

"Nothing," he said. "Just . . . butt sex."

"How old are you?" Anna asked him, but even Mom was laughing now.

Mom was way more real with me and my friends, about everything, really, compared to Anna's mom (her dad lived with his husband in Texas [which was one more thing you weren't supposed to talk about in front of her mom]) or either of Wexler's parents. But that also meant having some number of conversations you'd rather not have. It was a double-edged sword.

"In any case, I hope you guys are being careful," Mom said.

"We are," Anna told her.

Sorry, I mouthed, but Anna waved it away. She didn't care.

"And I hope you're not forgetting your friends, either," Mom added.

"What do you mean?" Wex asked.

"It's just a thing that happens," Mom said. "Romance blossoms, and all of a sudden, you don't want to spend time with anyone but each other."

"Mom." I appreciated where she was coming from, but in a mortified kind of way.

"I'm just saying." Mom flipped the new batch of french toast and pressed down to make it sizzle in the pan. "It's a thing. It's totally understandable, but it doesn't hurt to bear in mind."

"They're right here. *With me*," I said. "It's all good."

Close enough anyway. I mostly just wanted Mom to shut up.

"I'll say no more," Mom said, and loaded her own breakfast onto a plate, then came to sit down.

"Don't worry about him," Anna said to Mom, and squeezed my arm. "He couldn't get rid of us, even if he wanted to."

I smiled. It was a sweet thing to say, even if it wasn't entirely true.

Chapter 7

5:40

"Listen, don't get mad," I told Gina in the car on the way to my meeting that Thursday, "but I was kind of hoping you'd let me get you out of bringing me back to the lab after this."

"What's that supposed to mean?" she asked.

I'd gotten as far as asking her to drive both ways, but I hadn't worked up the nerve to ask her about the rest—about Swift—mostly because I was afraid she'd say no. And now, the whole thing had gotten away from me, until winging it had somehow turned into the better (= only) option.

"I was kind of planning on hanging out with a friend after the meeting," I said.

"A friend?"

She was definitely learning to read me.

"A guy in my group," I said. "I just want someone I can talk to who isn't in my family and—no offense—doesn't work at the lab."

"None taken," she said. "But I'm not going to lie to your father, if that's what you're getting at."

"You don't have to," I said. "Just let me get you out of it. I'm not trying to put you on the spot. I'm just—"

"Putting me on the spot," she said.

"I'm sorry," I said again. "I really should have asked you sooner, but the truth is, I was afraid you'd say no, and I'm kind of desperate. I've never even been out with a guy before."

It was embarrassing to admit, but it was also true.

"So tell your dad," she said.

"That's complicated," I said. "He doesn't want me 'dating' anyone this summer, and that's not even what this is. It's just doughnuts. But Dad's so hyper about my accident, and all the reasons I'm here in the first place, I don't think he'd understand."

I knew Gina felt a little sorry for me, now that she'd had a chance to see how Dad and I operated around each other, but I wasn't sure if it was enough to bring her on board.

So I pulled my phone out, slowly, like unholstering a weapon, with no sudden moves.

"How about this?" I asked. "I'll call Dad, and if you hear me lying about anything, you can speak right up."

I could tell she wasn't going to say yes, but she didn't say no, either, so I hit Dad's number and put it on speaker.

"What's up?" he answered. "Everything okay?"

"Gina is going out with friends later," I told him. That was true. I knew it from earlier in the day. "Technically she has enough time to get me back to the lab, but do you care if I take the bus?" I kept my eyes on Gina the whole time so she could watch me not (exactly) lying.

Dad paused. I had no idea if he was thinking about me or if he was working on something else.

"Dad?" I asked.

"Just call a car," he said.

"Can you tell Gina it's okay? She still looks uncomfortable," I said, which was also true.

"Thanks, G," Dad said. "It's fine. I don't want to hold you up."

"You're not," she said.

"Have a good night," he said, flexing those superior listening skills. "And, Chris, get a receipt, please."

After I hung up, Gina was conspicuously quiet, for Gina.

"Thanks," I said, to fill the silence as much as anything. It wasn't an ideal situation, but I'd also realized somewhere along the way that while I'd do whatever I could to get Gina on my side, it was never going to be as much as I was willing to do to hang out with Swift after that meeting. If I had to, I'd come clean with Dad at some point. But not now. Not yet.

So the fact that Gina never actually responded didn't really matter. Because this was happening either way.

5:55

Before the meeting, a bunch of us were standing around the refreshment table (aka the coffee, seltzer, pretzels, and sometimes baked goods table) eating pretzels when Danny came up and stood conspicuously next to me.

"You said your dad works at UC?" he asked me. "Is he that Schweitzer guy?"

"Yeah," I said.

"He's famous, right?" he asked.

I could feel people noticing the conversation. "Not exactly," I said.

"But he's a genius," Danny said, no question mark this time.

"So they tell me," I said. "Yeah."

"What's the name of that book?"

"The Weakness of Gravity," I said. It was Dad's bestseller from about two years earlier. Supposedly, it was going to be some kind of PBS series. Dad had a TV agent now and everything.

"Cool," Danny said, and looked at Swift but pointed at me. "This guy's father is the shit in physics."

"Wow, Danny, just put him on the spot why don't you?" Swift said.

I didn't mind, though. I wasn't sure what Swift might be thinking, but as far as I was concerned, it was all a win-win.

Swift was talking to me		
AND		
He was impressed that I had a famous father.	OR	He didn't care who my father was.
So I was good either way.		

"You still want to get shitty doughnuts?" I asked him then.

"Huh?" he said, and I felt immediately stupid. He didn't

even remember mentioning it the week before. It was just some piece of verbal litter he'd thrown down, and I'd mistaken it for flowers.

"Oh, you mean after the meeting?" he asked.

So, okay, he remembered, but it meant so little, he had to be reminded about it, whereas I'd spent the past seven days thinking about what kind of doughnut I was going to get, and what we were going to talk about, and how much it might cost if the two of us decided to go to Mexico that winter.

"Yeah," I said. "No big deal if you have other plans."

"No," he said. "My plans were to hang with you."

And not even I could come up with something bad to say about that. This just kept getting better and better for some reason.

"Sounds good," I said, and we headed over to the circle of chairs, where I assumed we'd sit next to each other. Which we did.

"So I'll see you then," I told him. "Have a good time at your meeting."

That got a smile. The first one of my very own.

"You too," he said.

7:01

I didn't say much at the meeting. I was still embarrassed about the week before and more than a little trigger-shy when it came time for sharing. Plus, my mind kept snapping back over to Swift. And doughnuts. And doughnuts with Swift.

Finally, the hour was up and Martina let us go—but then called my name before I could get out of there.

"Talk to you for a second?" she asked.

"I'll meet you outside," Swift said, and kept moving, while I went to see what Martina wanted.

"So what do you think?" she asked. "You've been to three meetings. Do you feel like you're getting anything out of this?"

"*I am,*" I said, enthusiastically to make up for the two-syllable answer. The clock was ticking on my doughnut time.

"I'll be honest," she said. "I've been wondering if this group is a good fit for you. I know last week was kind of rough—"

"No. It's okay," I said. Four syllables. Efficiency was key.

"Well, good," she said. I rocked back on my heels to leave. "I'd hate for you to measure whatever you get out of this against what someone else is meant to get out of it."

I exhaled. I flattened my feet again.

"Can I be honest?" I asked.

"Please," she said.

"I don't feel like I have a drug problem," I said. "I know you've probably heard that a million times, but I graduated with a decent GPA, I got into the school I wanted to get into—"

"You mean the school that you might not get to go to? Because of drugs?" she asked.

"Because of whippets," I said.

Now it was Martina's turn to take a beat and reset.

"Listen," she said. "Whatever else is true, your substance use landed you here. And by that, I mean in this group, but also in a place where you don't want to be for the summer. The question is, what do you want to do with that? In my experience, if you don't pay the early invoices, the price just keeps going up."

"Wait. Are we talking about drugs? Or are you talking about me and my dad?" I asked.

She opened her hands, palms up in a little shrug. "I can't answer that for you," she said.

I doubted that was true, but didn't say so. I just nodded and waited for her to finish—then realized she already had.

"So, are we all set?" I asked, and thumbed over my shoulder, then took a step back like my thumb was *that* heavy. "I think my dad might be waiting for me out there."

"Sure," she said. "Go ahead. I'll see you next week."

A second later, I was out the door.

7:05

When I got outside, Swift was checking his phone in the middle of the sidewalk. He looked up and saw me, and smiled, just before I spotted Gina's red Kia. It was parked about six spaces away from the place she'd dropped me off an hour ago. And there she was, leaning out the window with her elbows on the sill like that car was a little house she lived in.

"Hey," she said.

"What are you doing?" I asked, coming over. Swift looked up and watched us, but stayed where he was.

"I called your dad and said my plans got pushed and that I didn't mind taking you back to the lab one bit," she said.

"No," I said, closer now. "What are you *doing*?"

She looked me right in the eye. "I'm doing what I'm doing," she said. "What are *you* doing?" It wasn't aggressive, and she didn't seem mad. It was just confidence, which for Gina was like soup of the day. She always had it.

"Same thing, I guess," I answered.

"Okay then," she said, like it was settled. In other words, she wasn't going to let me just go off with some guy, but she wasn't going to tell Dad about it, either.

"Hey there, I'm Gina," she said to Swift next, and stuck her hand out of her little house to shake.

"I'm Swift," he said, coming over.

"As in Jonathan?" she asked.

"Not really. Just Swift. My parents made it up."

"Well, it's an interesting name. And nice to meet you," she said.

"Are you from Gisomo Hills?" Swift asked.

Gina shot me another look, not even trying to hide how much she loved that it wasn't her holding us up anymore.

"Marionville," she told him. "It's way nicer here."

"Marionville is nice, too," Swift said.

"That's what nice people say," Gina said, and winked. "But thanks anyway."

"Okay, half an hour, then," I butted back in, and checked my phone. "Starting now."

Gina gave me a familiar smile, like there was nothing in the world that could bother her, because God, and because Jesus, and because the blip of a human lifetime compared to the eternal happiness waiting on the other side, not maybe, but definitely. For her.

"Okeydoke," she said. "Starting now."

7:10

I got a cinnamon roll and a large coffee. Swift got a dozen doughnut holes, including the nasty jelly-filled ones that unfortunately touched the others in the box. I passed when he offered me one.

"So, what's your deal?" I asked. "What else do you do besides this group?"

"This summer? I work for my dad," he said. "I literally spend all day filling up shipping cartons with foam packing material. It's incredibly fascinating."

I smiled down at my plate. "Sounds like it," I said.

"You have no idea."

And I smiled again. All I wanted to do was smile.

"What are you shipping?" I asked.

He shrugged, presumably to indicate how much the answer didn't matter. "Computer parts. Board components."

"Oh," I said.

Deer. Headlights. I wasn't off to a very interesting start.

"What about you?" he asked.

"I do office stuff," I said, and echoed his shrug. "Data entry, filing, setting up equipment."

"What kind of equipment?" he asked.

"Physics," I said.

"So you work for your dad, too," he said.

"Yeah," I said, and now I felt stupid for hiding something so obvious. "We have a kind of complicated relationship."

"Me too," Swift said.

Speaking of me too . . .

"So, I want to ask you something," I told him, getting up my nerve once and for all. "I think I know the answer, but it's kind of embarrassing. Or at least it might be, if I'm wrong."

He narrowed his eyes in a way that looked sexy on him, but just would have made me look confused. "I'm thinking the answer is yes," he said, "but go ahead."

"Are you . . ." I stopped again. *Gay* seemed like the wrong word. Or maybe just the wrong thing to say. "Are you into guys?" I tried instead.

"See that?" he said. "I must be psychic."

In other words—yes. I wasn't surprised, but I was relieved to be sure.

I let it all sink in for a second and ate some cinnamon roll, then some more, biding my time on the dry outer circle, saving the tenderloin for when I'd spiraled my way in there.

"You're right, though," I said, holding up a piece. "They are kind of shitty."

There was a much better place about a mile from there, he

said, and suggested we check it out sometime, which I said sounded like a great idea.

And he'd been busted for something called Green, which was synthetic weed, which I'd never heard of before, but his college wasn't going to let him come back without some kind of counseling. Which also sounded familiar.

And I told him about my accident behind the restaurant in a lot more detail than I'd shared at the second meeting. He thought it was hilarious, in just the right way.

And about sixteen seconds later, half an hour had passed, and Gina was pulling up outside the doughnut shop. She waved at me through the window and pointed at the place on her wrist where she wasn't wearing a watch.

I waved back so she'd know I'd seen her, and also so she wouldn't come in.

"I have to go," I said.

"You always have to go," Swift said. It was like an accusation, but also a little like he was grabbing onto me and pulling me closer. Which was nice.

"I'm sorry," I said. "I suck."

"Don't say that."

Gina waved again.

"I better go."

"Can I kiss you?" he asked.

.

.

It felt like lightning at the back of my neck. The kind that brings monsters to life, as opposed to striking people dead.

I probably had coffee breath, didn't I? But then, so would

he. And Gina was watching, I realized. But I just. Couldn't. Make. That. Matter.

"Is that a no?" he asked.

"Oh, sorry. I kind of thought it was obvious. Yes, please," I said, and he leaned across the table.

His breath did smell like coffee, and his face was warm, and he was kissing me then. I could feel it on my lips, but also in my chest and my gut, like some kind of depth charge he'd dropped right through me. I wondered if Gina was watching, or if anyone else was for that matter, and then Swift sat back again, and it was over.

Wait. What?

It was like it had happened in negative time. Now it was all rushing away from me as fast as it had rushed up. I didn't even want to say anything, because words were just going to put more distance between me and that kiss.

"You okay?" he asked.

"Yeah. I'm good."

He couldn't have possibly known about the wild overdrive my mind was running in just then. I'm not sure anything better had ever happened to me before, and I don't mean that in a pathetic way. It was all so unlikely, from the ground up, that it felt like I'd broken some law of the natural universe. Like kissing Swift had meant getting away with something big and unexplainable.

"So, does your dad let you go out?" he asked.

"Good question," I said. "That's kind of a work in progress." Meanwhile, Gina was sitting right there in plain sight, and even though I hadn't asked her to do this (just the opposite, in fact), it was still kind of obnoxious of me to keep her waiting. "But I really better go—" I said.

"Thanks for coming out," he said.

"Absolutely. Talk to you soon?"

"I hope so," he said, with that calm confidence I couldn't even touch.

And whether I'd made Swift happen somehow, or just dumb-lucked into him, or if some version of myself had FedExed him to me from across the great divide, I had no idea. I just knew that I was glad for it, and that the only thing I wanted now—the only thing I could imagine ever wanting again—was more of the same.

Chapter Seven

9:05

When Mitch asked what I was doing after work that night, I'm pretty sure he thought I was going to say what Wexler, Anna, and I were doing, since that was my default.

But Wexler and Anna were going to just do Wexler and Anna that night, Anna had told me. And when I'd said to Wexler at the end of his shift, *So, I'll catch up with you tomorrow?* he'd said, *Ye-eah*, drawing out the word like he hadn't thought about it yet (even though he had to have), and like that sounded good, now that I mentioned it.

It was the first whole night I wasn't invited with them, which was inevitable, and totally understandable, and also impossible to miss.

"I'm just going to go home, probably," I told Mitch. "Maybe over to Eddie's. I don't know."

"You want to hang out?" he asked me.

Really?

It was a fast, pump-the-brakes kind of moment. We'd

never hung out before, not even in a group, and as far as I knew, that was by mutual agreement.

So what was this? The timing seemed too conspicuous for Mitch to think I wouldn't notice. And there wasn't enough room inside the natural rhythm of a conversation to weigh all the possibilities.

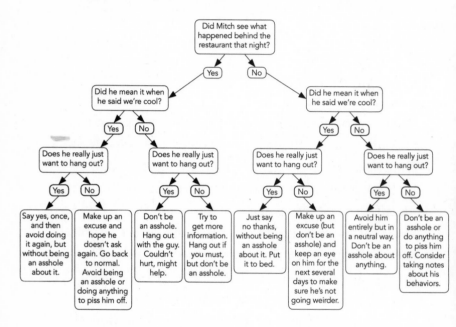

So I just went with it.

"Um . . . I guess," I said.

"Don't let me force you," he came back.

"No," I said. My brain was catching up to the situation, and it seemed like it had the potential to be a good idea. That insurance adjuster still had eighteen days to approve or deny my claim with the restaurant, so at a minimum, it couldn't hurt to play nice with Mitch until then.

Besides, it wasn't like I had anywhere else to be that night.

"Sure. I'm closing," I said. "So after that."

"I'll hang out," he said.

11:15

Mitch had terrible posture. It's not the kind of thing I usually notice, but I noticed his. It was like his shoulders were always fighting gravity, and always losing.

His car was a pit, too. The backseat looked like someone had unpacked from a long road trip—clothes, shoes, empty cups, broken-backed books, a bike rack that belonged on the outside of the car, and I don't know what else underneath all of that. The glove compartment was wired shut, and right now, he was rolling a joint in the gutter of a *National Geographic* magazine that he'd pulled out from under the driver's seat.

"Can I ask you a personal question?" I asked.

The outside of his right eye squinted shut, like he was cutting off his view of me.

"Why?" he asked.

"I'm just curious," I said. "Were you really in a cult?"

He took a breath then and puffed out his cheeks on the exhale. I could already tell that I was wrong about how it might be refreshingly honest of me to ask. But I really was curious.

"It wasn't a cult," he said. "But close enough, yeah. A church."

He finished rolling the joint between his fingers, bit off one end, and spit the tip out the window. Then he lit up and inhaled.

"'Ere," he said, holding his smoke and offering me a hit.

"No thanks," I said.

He kind of pulsed it at me then, offering more insistently. His expression read something like *Don't be a pussy*. And since I was probably going to reek anyway, just from sitting there, and since that joint felt as close to a literal peace pipe as he and I were going to get, I took a hit. Followed by a long, uncomfortable silence while we sat there holding our smoke.

It wasn't until I blew my hit out the window that I really looked around. And that's when I realized. This was exactly the view Mitch would have had when I passed out that night. I could see the back door of the restaurant and the concrete pad where it had happened, just like he would have seen. Assuming he was there. Which I pretty much had to assume. The real questions were: What, if anything, did he plan on doing with that information? And what, if anything, did it make sense for me to do about it in the meantime?

"If you really need to know," he said, "it's this church my dad belongs to. Everyone says it's a cult, which it's not, but it's pretty fuckin' close, and my mom hired some guy to go with her and pull me out of there. It wasn't pretty."

He shrugged then, like he'd run out of details as fast as he'd started talking about it.

I exhaled. "Was that against your will?" I asked. "When your mom took you?"

"Oh yeah," he said. "But I'm glad now." And we both went silent again. He took one more hit and put the joint out in a Snapple cap on the dashboard.

I could already feel the buzz coming on and got distracted, imagining myself passed out over there on the cement, while I also sat in Mitch's car, watching the scene play out, with the ambulance pulling up and Wexler yelling down at me.

Hang on, man. You're going to be okay.

"You okay?" Mitch asked.

"I'm good," I said.

It was a lie. My high had already come to that fork in the road and turned decisively paranoid. Between the general weirdness of being alone with Mitch and the fact that someone could come out that back door at any second, and also remembering my accident, it felt like everything had sped up to make way for all the thoughts, which were becoming unmanageable. The floodgates were open now, and I was wondering how I'd ended up out here, even though I knew. The inward spiral of it kept knotting, tighter and tighter, in my chest.

Mitch grinned at me. "It's good shit, right?" he said.

I was jealous. He didn't seem paranoid at all. And he probably had no idea how weirded out I was, either. He was like the opposite of me, including the fact that, between the two of us, he had nothing to lose.

"Yeah," I said. I took a deep breath and shook it off. Tried to shake it off.

"What kind of church is it?" I asked. I was asking too many questions, but it was easier than coming up with anything else to say. I just wanted Mitch to do most of the talking. Although by the same token, the longer this went on, the harder it was getting for me to pay attention. I was going to have to leave soon. I'd walk home, get up early, and come back for my car.

Also, I realized, I had no idea what Mitch had just said.

"Oh. Wow," I answered anyway. "I, um . . . hope everything's going to be okay."

Whatever he'd said before, he shrugged now. "I've gotta piss."

He was up, out, and behind the dumpster before I had to say anything else.

This was my chance to go, I realized. Mostly I'd been sitting there, figuring out how to extract myself from that car, and from Mitch in general.

But then something else hit me all at once.

This was my chance to *do something*, like Wexler had suggested. Something about Mitch. With my camera. Exactly the kind of thing I said I wasn't going to do. But now might.

And now was.

It was like my hands turned on the camera before my conscience could weigh in. I knew what I was doing, and I knew why I shouldn't, but now that I'd broken the seal on this thing, I couldn't (well, okay, didn't) stop.

I panned around to get a shot of the roach in the Snapple cap and the bag of weed on the seat, making sure to get enough of the car that there could be no mistake about whose it was.

Already he was coming back, and I should have clicked off at that point, but still didn't. Instead, I left the camera running and put it facedown on my leg.

When Mitch got in the car, we both just sat there for maybe half a minute. Silence never seemed to bother Mitch, and I forced myself to wait so it wouldn't seem too conspicuous. Then—

"Do you get high back here during your shifts?" I asked.

He let out something that could have passed for a cough, but I think was a laugh. "It's the only way to do eight hours on grill," he said. "This place *sucks*."

I felt terrible. Just not terrible enough to stop. Some part of me kept thinking, *Don't be stupid*, but even there, I wasn't sure if that meant *stop* or *go on*.

Stop.

Go on.

Stop.

Go on.

"Just weed?" I asked.

"You know," he said. "A little speed, a little coke if I can get it, but that means driving all the way back to Richmond."

Stop.

Go on.

"I don't know anyone who does coke," I said.

"So I guess that means you're not the biggest criminal around here after all," he said.

Stop.

I'd have to edit out that last part about me, but that was easy enough. Unless I decided to erase the whole thing, in which case it wouldn't matter. I was too stoned to be definitive about anything right now, and I just wanted to get out of there. So I slid my phone into my pocket, still running, and put my hand on the door handle.

"I think I'm gonna take off," I said.

"Where are you headed?"

"Just home," I said. My voice was gravelly, too heavy to lift out of my lungs. I cleared my throat and tried again. "I'm a-gonna walk." I have no idea why I said *a-gonna*.

"You want a ride?"

"I'm good," I said. *I'm a-good*. "You should just hang out here for a little while before you drive," I said. "Or walk, too. You smoked more than me."

Mitch pulled a pair of headphones out from the console between us and plugged them into his phone. Then he shook out a Camel Light, twirled it between his fingers, and stuck it in the curve of his upper lip, holding it there like a pencil. Maybe it was just the paranoia talking, but everything he did reminded me of a predator playing with its kill before dinner.

"Yeah," he said. "Not going home, that's for sure."

11:48

I was too stoned to see Mom, if there was any chance she might still be up. So I started walking, and took the very long way around. Somehow, I ended up on a bench in the middle of downtown, which was mostly closed up for the night.

I sat there and looked at the video I'd taken in Mitch's car. It was only a couple of minutes, most of it black screen with our voices in the background. But it was definitely incriminating enough to do something with, if it came to that.

What I really wanted to do was talk to Wex. This was his idea to begin with, which either made him the exact right or wrong person to tell me what to do next. So I texted him a copy of the whole thing.

Hey . . . I took your advice. Check it out. Now what???	

Part of me was hoping Wex and Anna were still out somewhere, and might even drive through town and see me. It was a little pathetic to hang my hopes on that, but it kept me sitting on that bench all the same.

The longer I sat, the more crowded my head got, thinking about Mitch and what I'd done, but then about Wex and Anna too, until they'd come fully front and center. The fact that those two weren't with me—and even more, the reasons why not—made me feel worse than I already did.

I needed to get some of this out, one way or another. So I opened a new text to both of them and just started typing.

Hey. I hope you guys won't mind, but I need to get something off my chest.
 	
    I just want to tell you that the last couple of weeks have been harder for me than I've been letting on. I feel like the three of us came all this way, since freshman year, and now, just at the end of everything, you two have split off into a separate unit, which sucks. For me, anyway.
 	
    I don't mean to make this all about myself. I just haven't found a way to say any of it out loud, and now I'm stoned and sitting here and (lucky you) vomiting it all up. Watch out for your shoes.
 	
    If I'm really honest, part of me wishes you guys were a little sorrier about this than you are, or at least that you could give a better impression of caring about what it all means for me. I don't know if that makes me selfish or just human, but it's how I feel.		

It seems like you're not thinking about it at all. And maybe that's because you just assume I'm fine with it. Or maybe it's because if things were the other way around, you wouldn't be bothered by it the same way I am. I'm not that good a person, which is a big part of what all this has shown me.

I know this is my problem. I guess I just wish it felt a little more like our problem. That's all. I love you guys. I really do. But I also really miss you.

It took me at least half an hour to write all that, read it, edit it in about twenty different ways, and then read it again. At some point, I started to realize I wasn't ever going to send it, but I kept going anyway.

When it felt finished, I read it three more times through, just to file it in my brain in case I ever wanted it back.

Then I did the same thing to that text that I'd done to Dad's letter four years earlier. I burned it in the bathroom sink. By which I mean, I deleted it and emptied the trash.

Same difference. It was gone now.

At least to the extent anything like that ever can be.

12:51

The next afternoon, Wex picked me up at home and I rode with him to the big Lowe's in Starkville for some kind of special light bulb his mom wanted. There was no way I was going to dredge up the whole thing about him and Anna, but he'd seen the Mitch video I'd sent, so there was plenty to talk about.

"I'm not going to lie," he said. "I'm surprised. I didn't think you were up for something like that." If anything, he sounded proud—of me, but also, maybe, flattered that I'd taken his suggestion.

"It just kind of happened," I said. "But I'm thinking maybe I should erase it."

"Why?" he asked. "Now that you have it, there's literally no reason to get rid of it."

"Um, ethics?" I said.

Wex seemed unconvinced. "I don't see how it hurts to just hold on to it. I mean, if you feel bad about doing it in the first place, that's kind of behind you now. Ethically, the damage is done."

I guessed so. Yes and no.

"Mitch really seems okay to me," I said. "Weird, but not vindictive, you know?"

"Mitch seems like he could be a lot of things," Wex said. "That's why I'd keep it."

He wasn't wrong about that, either. The news is full of people who *seemed* harmless, right up until they weren't anymore. Arguably, this whole thing was about which one of two people Mitch might be—the awkward but harmless guy; or the simmering, unpredictable guy with the invisible rubber band in his brain that could snap at any time without warning.

Which meant a standoff between my guilt and my paranoia. And so far, the paranoia was winning. Which made me feel guilty.

"If you're not sure, just wait," Wex said. "That's the whole point of insurance. You hope you never have to use it, but then you're glad it's there if something happens."

It was getting hard to tell where Wexler's logic left off and my own picked up. It was all fairly convincing, but maybe just because I wanted it to be. If nothing else, it was true that keeping the video for now left my options open. Erasing it didn't.

"Yeah, okay," I said. "I'm going to sit on it."

"That's what I'd do," Wex told me. He was just pulling into a McDonald's parking lot. "Come on. I'm starving. You want anything?"

Easiest question I'd had all day.

"Obviously," I said.

Chapter 8

9:45

Here's what I didn't see coming. Getting kissed by Swift meant spending all kinds of time after that *not* getting kissed by Swift. It was like time I didn't even know existed, until it did. And now it was constant.

I'd be eating dinner, or talking to Gina, or brushing my teeth, and there it was again.

that kiss

I could still feel it in my gut—the depth charge it had sent through me, like some kind of sense memory every time it came to mind. It was embarrassing how often I thought about it, even if nobody knew it was happening. I was embarrassed for myself, but in the way that eating a whole box of Pop-Tarts is embarrassing, which is to say, also delicious.

I didn't even know Swift well enough to know if he

was worth all the infatuation. Not that I could turn it off. I was just fascinated by the shiny object of him, his *him*-ness, his Swift-ness. I kept thinking, *How did this happen?* Because if there was something I'd done, I wanted to know what it was. And then I wanted to bottle that shit.

The thing was, I had no idea how to handle it from here. Every time I thought about it, it just opened up the million ways I might (= probably would) screw this up. So now that shiny object had also become this fragile glass thing, ready to smash into a million pieces if I made one wrong move. I spent the weekend talking myself into and out of texting him. I wasn't sure why he didn't get in touch with me, but the fact that he didn't seemed like a sign I shouldn't. Or maybe should. But probably shouldn't.

And then he did.

It was Monday morning. I was sitting at my desk, alphabetizing student files (so much fun), when his text came in.

	Hey

As soon as I saw who it was, my chest went all warm and caramelly. I loved getting some kind of tangible evidence that I'd crossed Swift's mind. That I'd taken the form of thoughts in his head. It made me bigger somehow. Bigger than myself, including the self from thirty seconds earlier who didn't even know if Swift was thinking about him or not.

Now I knew.

Hi!	
	I was just thinking about you.

He could have said that at pretty much any time during the past five days, and my response would honestly have been the same.

Me too	
	What were you thinking?
That the other day was the most fun I've had since I came to CA	
	We're going to have to do something about that
About what?	
	If the most fun you've had so far was eating a doughnut . . .
Not talking about doughnuts. But you knew that already didn't you?	
	Still, you need to get out more
I wish	
	Can I help?

I stared at my screen, considering the options. Could he help? For sure, if I could swing it somehow.

"Hey, Gina?" I asked. "Do you mind if I take my lunch early?"

She stopped with her hands just off the keyboard, the way she always did. Then she looked at the phone in my hand, and I'm pretty sure I saw her suppress a little smile. Gina wasn't stupid.

"You don't answer to me," she said, and went back to typing. "You can take lunch whenever you want."

"You want me to bring you anything back?" I asked.

Then, very sweetly, actually, she swiveled three-sixty in her chair and tilted her head back to look at me as she went around. "Just you," she said.

"You know you're really cute sometimes?" I asked. It was a facet of Gina I never would have predicted the day I met her.

"Oh, please," she said. "You don't have to butter me up."

"No butter," I said. "For real. You're just . . . not like I expected you to be."

"How did you expect me to be?" she asked.

The first words to come to mind were *super Christian*. But in fact, I realized, that wasn't it. She kind of *was* super Christian, as far as I could tell. Just not in the way I would have thought.

"I don't know," I said. "Just different."

"Okay then," she said, and pointed at my phone. "Go on, don't let me keep you."

And my thumbs took me right back to Swift.

What are you doing right now?	

	Working but I can get away

Excellent.

Do you have a car?	
	Yeah

Even better.

How close are you to UC?	

11:24

Ninety-some minutes later, we were halfway through a large pepperoni at the student union. He'd driven over to meet me, and kissed me hello, right there on the front steps. It would have made me self-conscious back home, but as far as anyone here was concerned, I was just some guy who kissed other guys in public all the time. Which, technically, put me one step closer to actually being that guy.

Swift made it hard to worry, about anything really, except maybe that he'd get to know me well enough to realize I wasn't worth the trouble. But in the meantime, it was just me, him, my favorite food, and (at that moment) one of my favorite topics.

"Here's another thing," I said. "If everything is theoretically possible, then it's just as possible that in some of those possibilities I'm aware of me, here, in a way that I—me, here—can't perceive me, there. See?"

Swift had this calm sort of grin on his face, like he had no idea where this was going but he liked the ride all the same.

"Do you mean like we're being watched?" he asked.

"Sort of," I said. "Maybe we've spent all this time thinking about aliens watching us, when it's really ourselves on the other side of some cosmic one-way mirror. I'm here and he's there."

"He?"

"Me," I said. "Back in Ohio. Some version who didn't get busted and shipped out here by his father."

"Hmm," he said. Not in a bad way. Just taking it in. And then, "Am I allowed to say I'm glad you got busted? Because I like this version better."

I loved how he went there with me. So easily. So willingly.

"You're allowed," I said. "Asterisk, massive understatement."

Under the table, his foot slid up on top of mine. I pushed back, and he pressed harder, like he wasn't going anywhere even if I tried to make him. There was a tiny intensity to it that I loved.

"What time do you have to be back?" he asked.

Usually I took forty-five minutes for lunch, and I'd already been gone almost an hour.

"Why?" I asked. "What did you have in mind?"

Swift leaned in and lowered his voice. "I was thinking maybe we could go make out in my car," he said—and all that warm caramel in my chest morphed into a ball of exclamation points.

"How can I say no to that?" I asked.

"The question is, why would you want to?" he asked.

And, of course, I couldn't think of a single reason.

11:31

We got as far as the men's room. I went in for a pit stop, and by the time I'd turned around to wash my hands, Swift was standing there by the sinks.

He grabbed me when I came close enough and kissed me. The student union was summer empty, so there wasn't much chance of anyone coming in. And I only sort of cared if they did.

He hadn't shaved. I liked the sandpaper, and I was smiling when we pulled apart.

"What is it?" he asked.

"Nothing," I said, and rubbed his cheek. "Just this."

When he kissed me again, he turned us one-eighty and backed me up a step. My shirt got soaked against the edge of the sink, but I didn't care about that, either. I was making out. With a guy I actually liked. A lot.

Physically speaking, it wasn't so different from that one time mashing face with Andy Goldreyer's cousin (Owen? Ethan?); hands on each other's arms and backs, mouth to mouth, tongue to tongue.

Still, it felt like a completely different experience. It felt like getting paid back for every unrequited crush I'd ever had, all in one easy installment. Like after a lifetime of shouting into some unresponsive void, I was finally getting back the echo I'd been waiting for.

Hello!

    Hello!

I'm here!

    Me too!

And for those next twenty minutes, even in that fluorescent-lit tiled box of a bathroom, all I knew was that I was exactly where I wanted to be, doing exactly what I wanted to be doing, with exactly the person I'd want to do it with. All without exactly *wanting* anything at all.

Flow. That's what some people call it. Flow. And it wasn't just theoretical anymore. It was happening. This. Him. Us. Now. All of it completely real.

11:53

I didn't want it to end, but it was already late.

"I hate this," I said. I left my hand on Swift's hip, just above his pocket. "I don't want to go."

"I don't want you to," he said. "We haven't even tried the hand dryer yet."

It was a little sad that he made me laugh so easily, only because I had to leave.

"What are you doing this weekend?" he asked. "Is your dad still keeping you locked up?"

"Well, yes," I said, "But even if he weren't, he's actually getting married on Saturday."

"Married?" he asked, as in, *You're just now mentioning this?*

"It's just a small thing at the house," I said. "Second time for both of them."

"Oh, so you *don't* have to be there," he said without missing a beat.

I leaned the top of my head into his chest and left it there, like one part cuddling and one part banging my skull against a wall.

"You have no idea how tempting that is," I said.

"Well, I'll see you at the meeting on Thursday if that counts for anything," he said.

"I'm hoping Gina will hang out again. I still have to talk to her about it."

"You do that," Swift told me, and I finally dragged myself out of there once and for all, but not until I'd made sure to give him one last kiss goodbye. Five more times.

Then, as I headed outside and started walking back across the campus, a new question floated into my mind. Something I'd never gotten to ask myself before.

Did I have a boyfriend?

And since I didn't know the answer, and since I was in such a good mood, and felt like cutting myself a break, I thought—

Let's just say yes. For now.

12:17

I looked up from my desk a little while after I got back, and Dad was standing there, holding a blue folder. I wondered if he'd been waiting for me to notice him, or if he'd just come in.

"We have a colloquium next Wednesday and I'll want coffee and all the usual for twenty people," he said, handing over the folder. "Gina, can you tell him how to order everything?"

"Yepper."

It was vaguely insulting that Dad thought I hadn't figured out this process by now. But then again, Dad couldn't remember my birthday most years. If anything, I wish he'd been a little *more* clueless, because what came next was—

"And, Chris? How long were you at lunch?"

Which was a tricky question. In a perfect world, it wouldn't have mattered if Dad knew about Swift or not. Dad was a lot of things, but he wasn't a homophobe.

Meanwhile, though, back in my imperfect world, coming clean would have meant

| Admitting my original lie, that Swift was straight, |
| even if it wasn't technically a complete lie when I told it, given that I wasn't sure about Swift myself at the time, |
| which was too nuanced a point to be useful against Dad |
| (*especially* Dad), |
| not to mention, if he was going to start calling me out on this, I didn't trust myself with what I might say in response, |

not because it might hurt him in some way
but because I couldn't afford the conflict, given everything else I had to lose,
starting with Swift
and ending with Birch.

It was too many layers, and too many moving parts. I couldn't risk it.

"Sorry about that," I told Dad. "I had my camera out and I guess I just lost track of time." It was as credible as anything else I could say.

"Well, just make sure it's reflected on your time sheet," he said. "And don't make a habit of it, okay? It's not fair to Gina."

"It was no problem," Gina said.

"Maybe not this time," Dad said. "But everyone needs to pull their weight around here."

"Sorry, Gina," I said.

She just looked at me without a word, until Dad was gone again. Then she wheeled over and put her elbows on my desk.

"Everything okay?" she asked.

"Yeah, fine," I said. "Just complicated."

"Then maybe you should tell him," she said.

"That's the complicated part," I said.

"Well . . ." She sat up straight and looked me in the eye. "Just so you know, I don't think I can help you with this anymore."

"What do you mean?" I asked. I didn't know what she was going to say, but I knew I wasn't going to like it.

"I mean, what just happened here? With your dad? It's not *like* I'm lying to him. I *am* lying to him. And I can't keep doing that," she said.

"Okay," I said slowly, trying to take it all in. Gina was one of the few limbs I had to lean on here, and now it looked like she was amputating herself right out of the picture. "What about everything you already know? Everything that's already happened?" I asked.

"That's between us," she said. "I told you that you could trust me about all that, and I meant it. But from now on, if there are secrets you need to keep from your dad, I don't want to know about them. It's too uncomfortable for me."

I was fighting back a little panic, and the next question came out before I could stop myself.

"Is this because Swift is a guy?" I asked.

I knew it was a mistake as soon as I'd said it.

Gina looked at me like I'd burped in her face. "You know what? Screw you," she said. Then she swiveled to her own desk and turned her back on me.

Now my heart was really kicking. I didn't have any context for dealing with angry Gina. She'd always been so impervious to everything I said, I didn't even know I had the option of pissing her off. Not that I'd ever wanted to.

"I'm sorry," I said. "I didn't mean that."

"I think you did," she said without looking over. "You're just like your father, you know that?"

"What do you mean?"

"Well, *you're welcome,* for starters. You jerk."

It was like a slap, coming from her. I felt terrible, and not just for the last sixty seconds, but all of it.

"I thought we were friends," I said, not even sure what I meant.

"I know you did," she said. "But think about it. What have you done for me since you got here? What have you done for anyone but yourself?"

"Oh god, Gina. I'm really sorry," I said. "I wasn't thinking."

"Clearly," she said, shuffling some files around on her desk, keeping busy, not looking at me. "I'll drive you after work on Thursday, but your dad will have to pick you up, and you can tell him whatever you want about that."

I said the only thing I could.

"Okay."

I didn't know *what* to say. It was like she'd pulled away a curtain and showed me a whole view I hadn't even noticed before. But now it was about as missable as the Grand Canyon.

And about as fixable, too.

1:30

Hey, I'm not going to be able to hang out on Thursday. Gina changed her mind about all that. She's going to drop me off but my dad's picking me up.	
	Everything ok?
I screwed up with her, big time. I'll figure it out but it sucks meanwhile.	
	I can come to campus again if that helps. Same time tomorrow?
Sounds good. But this is getting ridiculous. I want to get out and actually do things in the world with you!	
	Anytime. Like what?
Well, besides the obvious :) I really want to see the ocean. We don't get too much of that in Ohio . . .	
	That can happen.

Thanks for being understanding. I know it's kind of weird.	
	It's fine. Don't overthink it.
Story of my life	

Chapter Eight

10:54

Now that everything was out in the open, Wexler and Anna didn't have any reason to spend their nights doing anything but each other, unless you counted hanging out with me, which sometimes they did and sometimes they didn't.

Basically, the volume of their sex life was inversely proportional to the number of nights I got to hang out with them anymore.

And by extension, it also correlated to the amount of time I had for damage control with Mitch. Usually that looked like me sticking around after my shift, watching him smoke behind the restaurant, listening to music in his car, and making small talk. Usually very small. Because Mitch.

It wasn't a friendship, exactly. More like a hangoutship with a purpose. Also a second, less sleazy insurance policy than the Untitled Mitch Mitchell Project I still hadn't erased from my phone.

So when Mitch's old Audi was in the shop one night and he asked me for a ride at the end of our shift, I told him he should come with me to Eddie's, if he wanted to. And Mitch surprised me by saying yes.

On our way over, he didn't do much to hold up his end of the conversation, but that was nothing new. The thing I was starting to figure out was that it meant I could pretty much talk about anything I wanted. And whatever this thing with Mitch was or wasn't, I couldn't help getting a little more curious about him every time we hung out. Once you scratched the surface, he didn't get any less weird, but he did get more interesting.

"So when you left that church, did they have to deprogram you or anything like that?" I asked.

He shrugged, but then answered. "I see a shrink once a week. There's a lot of stuff about reconciling how things might have been different if I hadn't spent the last three years with my dad. Stuff like that."

Once every several sentences, Mitch used words like *reconciling*. It had seemed incongruous at first, but now it was lining up with my revised sense of him.

"That's funny," I said. "I mean, not funny, but I think about that kind of thing all the time. Like what my life might have been like if X, Y, or Z were different."

Mitch didn't respond. It was like I hadn't spoken.

"Not that I'll ever know," I went on.

Still nothing.

It wasn't like I'd stopped feeling uncomfortable around him, but I was more comfortable with being uncomfortable, which was something, anyway, in Mitch World. So I kept going.

"You know what I don't get," I said, "is why you've been opening up to me like you have been all this time."

"Fuck off," he said.

"No, I'm serious," I said. "It was like after my accident, you seemed to come for me—"

"*Comfort you?*"

"*Come* for me," I said. "But then you started wanting to hang out."

"Oh," he said. He smiled, and then unsmiled. "I wasn't coming for you."

"Why were you so weird about it, then?" I asked.

"I don't know," he said defensively. "Maybe because I *am* weird?"

The self-awareness surprised me, and stumped me back into silence, too. I didn't try to come up with anything else. We were just pulling up to Eddie's house anyway.

Mitch got out first, and I took out my phone. I sat there with my feet on the pavement and my butt on the seat while I pulled up the video I'd made on that stupid night in his car.

I hit the little trash can on my screen.

DELETE VIDEO / CANCEL

"You coming?" Mitch asked.

"Hang on. I just got a text," I said.

I hit DELETE VIDEO.

I hit EMPTY TRASH.

I hit YES.

Then I pocketed my phone and went to catch up with him in the driveway. "I'm coming, I'm coming," I said. "You don't have to get hysterical about it."

I'm virtually certain he knew it was a joke, although with Mitch, you never can tell. Which, in its own weird way, meant I wasn't going to worry about it.

At least I got to be the funny one.

11:29

The last people I expected to see at Eddie's were Wexler and Anna. But there they were, sitting on the couch in Eddie's garage when Mitch and I got there.

"Hey!" Anna said. She pulled me down to sit next to her.

"What's up?" I said. It was a little weird to bump into them like a couple of acquaintances, but mostly because I was still stuck on the old me, the one who'd always known where Wex and Anna were, usually because I was there, too.

"We just thought we'd come see if you were around," Wexler said. That may or may not have been exactly true, but I was glad to see them.

"You guys know Mitch from the restaurant?" I asked the room.

Mitch either did or didn't pick up on the muffled surprise from everyone that he was there, but I saw it.

"Hey," Eddie said. "I'm Eddie."

"Hey," Mitch said. "Anyone want to smoke a bowl?"

So he knew at least one way to make friends, anyway. Eddie, Wexler, Jake, and Lainie all followed him right back outside to the yard, leaving me alone with Anna and Berylin. I'm pretty sure Eddie's parents were home, but the fact that I literally didn't know what either of them looked like said everything about why it didn't matter if they were there or not. We hung out at Eddie's a lot for that reason.

Berylin turned to me as soon as the others were gone.

"So . . . is he . . . ?"

"The cult guy? Yeah," I said. "He's okay."

"No," Berylin said, "I mean, are you two . . . ?"

"Oh," I said. "*No*. Definitely not."

I liked hanging with just the girls sometimes, even if Berylin did come in horns first. But she cared.

Anna and Berylin talked for a while about Berylin's job at the farm stand outside of town, and some guy named Rolf. I didn't absorb a lot of the details.

Then Berylin turned her attention back on me.

"When's your dad's wedding?" she asked.

"I leave tomorrow," I said.

"Are you excited?"

"He's not," Anna said.

Berylin reached over and picked a piece of skin off my nose with her fingernail. "You're flaking all over the place. You need to moisturize before this thing."

I pulled back out of reach. "Okay, thank you," I said.

"I'm not going to hurt you," she said.

"I didn't think you were," I told her, and cupped a hand over my nose. "It's just, he's been through a lot. He needs his rest."

"Okay, fine," she said. "Please tell him I'm sorry."

"He can hear you," Anna said. "He's right there."

That made me laugh—but then she kept going.

"It hasn't been that long since 'the accident,'" Anna said. "So you know, he's still kind of sensitive."

She'd put air quotes around the accident, and Berylin seemed to pick right up on it.

"Why is it 'the accident'?" Berylin asked.

I couldn't believe Anna had just done that. I tried to stay exactly as calm as I'd been two seconds ago, while she sat there looking a little vacant, and a little panicked herself.

"I don't know," she said. "It's just, we talk about it so much, it's become like this thing. Like, 'the accident.' You know?"

Berylin shook her head and whatever'd it away, while Anna flashed me a silent apology with her eyes. Not that I thought Berylin was some huge security risk. But it just drove home what I already knew—that this lie meant more to me than it ever would to Anna. Or Wex. I was the one who could lose his job. The one who'd have to answer to his parents. The one who needed the other two to stay invested.

"Seriously, though, why don't you ever have a boyfriend?" Berylin asked me, as if that had been the point from the beginning. "I know this town isn't exactly crawling with gay boys, but you're awesome. It's not like you have all these glaring flaws."

"No. Just lots of well-hidden ones," I said.

"So then . . . ?" she asked.

I thought about it for a second, and about whether I wanted to answer seriously or not.

"I guess if I knew why I didn't have a boyfriend, you wouldn't have to ask in the first place," I said.

"Well, maybe we need to find you one," she said. Somehow it sounded like a threat, coming from her.

"Find him a what?" Lainie asked. She'd just come back in.

"We were talking about getting Chris a boyfriend," Berylin said, while Lainie sat on the arm of the couch, and smiled down at me, and scritched my hair.

"I'll find my own, thanks," I said.

The others were filtering in. Mitch came over and sat on a lawn chair, across the coffee table from us. And just like that, he got folded into the room.

"Besides, he already has one," Anna said.

"Wait, what?" Berylin said.

"His name is Swift," Anna said.

"I've never heard of him," Berylin said. "Does he live in town?"

"He's theoretical, but he lives in California," I told her.

"Okay, I don't even know what that means, but *Swift*?" Berylin asked.

"I know," Anna said.

"That is a terrible name," Berylin said.

"It's kind of random, but it's too late to change now," Anna said.

"Except where it's not," I said, and we goofy-grinned at each other.

Berylin groaned. "You guys suck," she said. "You think it's entertaining, but it got old about two years ago."

Wexler held out a fist for a little across-the-room solidarity. "Preach," he said, and she air-bumped him back.

"It's not our fault we have a secret language," Anna said.

"Yeah, well, I wish it was a little more secret," Berylin said.

I couldn't help checking Mitch's reaction. I assumed he knew I was gay, but I had no idea if he cared, or knew I was maybe a little weird, too.

"So what's his story?" Mitch asked as soon as our eyes met.

"What?" I hadn't been expecting him to say anything.

"The guy with the bad name," he said.

"Swift," I told him, and then with huge fake indignity for the room, "His *name* . . . is *Swift*!" It got the laugh I was going for.

"And that's it?" Mitch said. "Just a name?"

"No," I said. "He could be anything."

"He could be everything," Anna said.

"Maybe he's got some kind of flesh-eating bacteria," Wexler said, just to give me a hard time.

"Or," I countered, "maybe I fall in love."

"*Aw*," Lainie said. "And maybe he has some big secret he's keeping, too."

"Like flesh-eating bacteria," Eddie said.

"Or like he's an alien!" Mitch said, a little too fast and a little too loud. Coming from someone else it might have been funny, but it just landed with a thud in the middle of the room. All of a sudden, Mitch was trying too hard, which was a weird color on him, in a vaguely sweet kind of way. I gave it a courtesy laugh to fill the silence, and the room moved on.

Then while everyone started talking about something else, Anna tapped me on the forearm and leaned into me.

"You're not in love with Swift, by the way," she said. "You're just infatuated."

"Oh, because you know?" I asked.

She shrugged. "I did kind of invent him."

"Come on," I said. "Let me have this. It costs you nothing."

"You don't need my permission," she said. "You can make it whatever you want."

It seemed like a needlessly ungenerous way to be, especially from someone who was having actual sex on a regular basis. I wanted to be mad, but even for me, that was one too many layers of crazy.

"Omigod, you are so boring," Berylin said. I didn't realize she'd been listening, but now she had the whole room's attention all over again. "I mean, let's say I take any of this seriously, which I don't. But if I did—why not just be here? This is our last summer together. You want to spend it talking about some life that doesn't exist?"

"Why not?" Eddie asked. "This town is boring as shit."

Berylin threw a cork at me to get me to look at her. "Just be *here*," she said. "How are you going to get an *actual* boyfriend if you're not even here?"

I threw the cork back. "I'm going to acknowledge the excellence of that question without answering it," I said.

I glanced over at Anna for backup, but she'd already turned her attention to Wexler, and I could see she was giving him the look.

The time-to-go look.

The *sex o'clock* look.

"I think we're going to take off," Anna said.

Berylin caught it, too, and she gave me a look of her own. Like *there they go again*. As in, Wexler and Anna, not me. I wasn't part of that *they* anymore. Now I was one of the everybody-else, watching them go.

This was the new living arrangement. It was like Wexler and Anna had moved out of the house we'd been sharing all this time and gotten their own place, *right next door*, where I was welcome, *anytime, anytime at all*, just as long as I didn't mind, *you know, maybe knocking* when I wanted to come over.

Because nothing had changed. Except for the parts that had.

11:48

I don't think I'd ever realized how much Wex and Anna defined me until that night. We'd always been this unit, scheduled to split into three equal pieces at the end of that summer. I'd never even considered the possibility of splitting in two, much less with me on the short side of that math. I'd always stupidly flattered myself that I was some kind of fulcrum between them, one of the guys with Wexler and one of the girls with Anna—the perfect friend, right up until they started looking to each other for the one thing I couldn't give either of them.

So when Wex said I should follow them out to his car, what I was really hoping for was something like

> *You know what we should do? Sleep out*
> *in the pine forest tonight.*
> *I like that. What about you, Schweitz?*

But it wasn't that. They just wanted to say goodbye.

"So, have a good time, if you can." Anna gave me a big hug by Wex's car and held on while she kept talking. "It's a wedding, sweetie. Try to love someone, even if it's not your dad."

It was good advice. Very Anna.

"You guys feel like staying out, by any chance?" I asked. My flight was at eight a.m., and I hadn't even started packing yet. Mom would be pissed, but I was willing to take it.

Wexler and Anna looked at each other, but not for long.

"Let's do something next week when you're back," she said.

"Sure," I said. "No problem."

What was I going to say? The fact was, I wanted them

to *want* to hang with me on the night before I took off, and before they'd have a whole weekend to themselves. That didn't seem like too much to ask. Just too much to ask out loud.

"Are you okay?" Wex asked. "You look like you're going to cry."

So I guess it showed.

It was like everything that had been building up, all the little ways I'd lost them over the last few weeks, was hitting me in one concentrated dose—a machete chop to recap a thousand paper cuts. I felt dismembered, while the two of them had been busy adding parts to themselves.

I tried to say "I'm fine," but a sob jumped off the *f* in "fine," and it came out as some embarrassing, wordless thing instead. The seal was broken now. I was definitely crying and I couldn't stop.

"Oh my god," Wexler said. "What is it?"

Not that this was anyone's fault. It wasn't even personal. I knew that. But I could know that all day and it didn't change the fact that I was still there with my hands on my knees, sobbing in front of them like an idiot.

Time folded around me, and even as I watched my own tears drip like disappearing ink into the pavement at my feet, I was conscious of the memorialization of this moment. From now on, this would always be The Night Chris Lost It In Front Of Eddie's House.

"Oh man, Schweitzy. Come here." Wexler put his arms around me and hugged me into a standing position. "You really don't want to go, do you?" he asked.

"No . . . ," I said, meaning *No, that's not why I'm crying.* But it also sounded like I was saying *No, you're right, I don't want to go.*

And then Anna was talking. "Come on, you'll be fine. I promise," she said, rubbing my back. "We'll see you in four days, and we'll talk constantly in the meantime. You know we will."

I wouldn't have thought there was room for one more thing in my brain, but it had all just shifted again. They didn't even know why I was upset. And I definitely didn't have it in me to back the whole thing up and explain now. It was too embarrassing. Almost as embarrassing as crying over this wedding. Which I wasn't, but I went with it.

"I'm fine," I said, and stepped back. "Sorry. Sorry. That was stupid." I was reining it in as fast as I could, and even felt a little relieved. I'd almost gone down the wrong rabbit hole, but not quite.

"Come out with us," Wex said.

"Don't worry about it," I said. "Seriously."

"Come *out*," he said. He put his fists up and lunged with his shoulder, kind of shadowboxing with me the way he did sometimes. But I never knew what to do with that. I just tensed, and he stopped, and it got even more awkward than it had already been.

"I can't," I said. "I'm Mitch's ride."

"Don't worry about that," Wexler said. "Someone else can take him home."

"I *have* to worry about it," I said.

— 199 —

"Chris is right," Anna said, maybe for reasons of her own, but there was no way I could stay out with them now. Not after all this. It wasn't even possible.

"How long do you have to keep being nice to him?" she asked.

"The insurance window closes tomorrow," I said. "Then they have to pay the claim, so I'll have the adjuster off my back. But it's not like I'm going to just stop talking to him."

"Right?" Wex said. "He could still get you fired after that. Or totally mess things up with your parents."

"That's not what I mean," I tried again. "I just . . . I don't know. I feel sorry for him."

"Come on," Wex said, trying to insist with me all over again. "You don't want to deal with *Mitch* right now, do you?"

"Don't worry about it," a voice said out of the dark. "I'm just going to walk home."

I looked over and saw Mitch's shadow at the top of the driveway, tall enough to clear the roof of Eddie's Jeep, even with the hunched shoulders.

I didn't know how much he had heard, but he wasn't coming any closer. He started cutting across the lawn instead, away from us and toward the street. Anna's hand was over her mouth. Wexler was looking from Mitch to me and back, like he was ready for whatever might happen.

"Mitch?" I asked. "Don't you want a ride?" I was still clinging to the possibility that he hadn't heard us, but he had. Of course he had.

"Mitch?" I tried again.

"Leave me alone."

"That wasn't like it sounded."

"I don't know what you're talking about," he said without stopping, so I started after him.

"Just hang on," I said.

He stopped short then and turned on me, fast enough that I flinched. I'd never been in a fight in my life, and I knew Mitch could wreck me if he wanted to.

"I told you to leave me alone. Which part of that didn't you understand?"

"I'm sorry!" I said. "Okay?"

"Oh, you're *sorry*," he said, nodding like it all made sense now. "And?"

"And?" I asked. I didn't understand the question. "I don't know. I'm just . . ."

Nothing. I was nothing. I felt like a piece of shit because I was one.

"What the hell does *sorry* do for me?" he asked. "I don't need it."

I still thought he might hit me, but I stayed where I was, only because I was afraid to move off of this moment, this piece of time, and into something even worse.

"Well, what *do* you need?" I asked. It sounded stupid out loud, but it was all I had.

"Nothing," he said. Both his hands went up like I was holding a gun on him, and he took a step back. "My mistake."

Then he turned and walked away again.

This time, I let him go. I just stood watching while he passed under a streetlamp and back into the dark. That's when he started running. I heard his feet on the pavement. A second later, he was around the corner and gone.

Fuck, fuck, fuck, fuck, fuck.

Chapter 9

12:12

Swift came to campus for lunch every day that week. I let Gina hold down the break room by herself and snuck off to the union, which was like our spot now. Dad literally never traveled that direction on campus, so I didn't worry about it too much.

As for Gina, things were civil, and cordial, and "fine," which was uncomfortable compared to how it had been before, but also not terrible. Just sort of gray. It wasn't like I needed another reason to love my midday Swift breaks, but they did keep me from having to navigate *not* eating with Gina anymore. Technically, where I went in the middle of the day was a secret now, for her sake as much as mine.

The hard part was making it back to my desk on time(ish) every day. Like whenever Swift and I said goodbye and I made that walk back to Moore Hall, I was leaving heaven for earth all over again. No wonder babies cry when they're born.

One day, Swift picked me up and drove me around Gisomo Hills. He showed me his high school, and we got huge sandwiches and milkshakes at the place where he used to hang out, and then ate them in his car. It was so simple. So awesome. So perfect.

"Thanks," I said.

"For what?"

"For making this summer bearable, and then some," I said. "And then some more."

"I think I'm coming out ahead on this one," he said.

"Yeah, right," I said. "Have you looked in the mirror lately?"

It was a joke, but he didn't smile. "Don't do that," he said.

"Do what?"

"Put yourself down. You do it a lot. And you're totally adorable, by the way."

Now I was flat-out embarrassed. Not that I wanted him to stop.

I'd never had conversations like these before. It was like I never could have, until now. Until Swift. And the fact that it took this long to get here seemed to make sense, somehow. All that waiting, all those years of wondering if (or when, or if) I was ever going to meet someone were nothing now. Just weightless thoughts in my brain. Years, collapsed into a single idea, or memory, pointing me toward this summer, and to him.

Swift got me. And when I was with him, I *was* me. I was more me than I'd ever felt before, and I never wanted it to stop. This was *something*. I could feel it. But Swift was the first one to say it out loud.

"So, are you my boyfriend?" he asked, when we got back to campus that day, and before I got out of the car.

"Let me check," I said. I rolled my eyes up and side to side like I was taking stock of something invisible. "I think I am," I said. "But how will I know for sure?"

He leaned over and kissed me on the lips then.

"Yep," he said. "Tastes like boyfriend."

"Oh, thank god," I said. "I was afraid I might taste like chicken."

7:40

I tried FaceTiming Wexler that night, and Anna picked up in his car.

"He's just getting something to drink," she said. I could see they were parked downtown.

"What are you guys doing?"

"Movie," she said.

"Just the two of you?"

"Yeah. Berylin's in Myrtle Beach and I don't know what Eddie's doing. I think he has some kind of family reunion, but I'm not sure. It's like nobody's around."

She was saying more than she needed to, I noticed. And just like that, I was out of reasons for not asking the question I wasn't asking.

"Is anything going on with you guys?" I said.

"What do you mean?" she asked. "I just told you—"

"No. I mean with you and Wex," I said. "You know."

"Oh," Anna said. "That. Oh. Wow. That's kind of a sudden question."

"Got it," I said, because she'd basically just answered.

She knew she had, too. "Do you feel weird now?" she asked me.

"No," I said. But obviously yes.

"Oh, shit. You do feel weird," she said. She'd already seen through me. "I'm sorry. We should have said something sooner."

It wasn't like I was shocked. More like I'd walked into the surprise party that I'd already been expecting. "Just give me a minute to catch up," I said. "This is kind of huge."

"I know, right?" she said. "Wex doesn't want you to feel bad, but I know you're a grown-up. You can take it. Don't tell him I told you, okay?"

"I won't," I said. "I'm just curious, though. How long has it been going on?"

I wasn't *just* curious.

"Honestly? Since a little before you left," she said.

That was right around the time Wexler told me it wasn't happening, and wouldn't happen, and that they'd tell me if it did. Which by then, I now knew, it had already started.

The whole thing was some combination of *not my business* and *completely my business*, and it left me not knowing what to say. Anna was telling me the truth to be a good friend, and Wexler was keeping it from me for the same reason. Which was weird, but not actionable.

So I changed the subject.

"Hey, guess what? I actually kind of met someone my-self," I said.

"No way!" she said. "Like a boy, with a penis and every-thing?"

"I don't know about that yet, but you can go ahead and be glad for me," I said.

"I am *so* going to go ahead and do that," Anna said. She'd jumped right on it, like the life raft it was meant to be. "How did you meet him?"

Then I heard Wexler get in the car.

"Schweitzy!" He was leaning into the screen now, right up against Anna, like in the video they'd sent me from Eddie's house. I wondered if he knew he was doing it.

"Tell me you're not drinking that blue shit again," I said.

"Okay, I won't tell you," he said, and took a long drink of it on camera for me to see. Then he over-burped for emphasis.

"Gross," Anna said, and left the frame while Wexler took over. I wondered if her mind was racing like mine, or if she'd already packed up our conversation and put it away. She could be cool like that. Including a little cold.

"Hey, guess what?" Wexler said.

"No, *you* guess what," Anna told him from offscreen. "Chris has a boyfriend."

That word still didn't feel like it belonged to me, but I liked getting to use it anyway—like driving a rented con-vertible.

"What?" Wexler said.

"Can you believe it?" I asked.

"Damn, you move fast," Wex said.

"I guess," I said. "If eighteen years and two months counts as fast."

"What's his name?" Anna asked.

"Swift."

"Seriously?"

"I kind of like it," I said.

"How did you meet him? In your drug thing?" Wexler asked.

"Ding ding ding."

I didn't want to jinx it, or make a big deal out of this before it felt a little more real to me. And I definitely didn't want to circle back to the Wex-and-Anna thing. So I kept dodging.

"But what were you going to say before?" I asked Wex.

"Oh, right!" he said. They were moving again, and I could see Anna was driving. That was new, too. Nobody ever drove Wex's car but Wex. "I was talking to Mitch Mitchell today, and supposedly he saw your whole accident," he told me.

"No way," I said.

"Yeah. The passing out, the ambulance, all of it. He said he was sitting in his car just watching the whole time. Stoned, probably."

"Is that the cult guy?" Anna asked from off camera.

"Yep," I said.

I hadn't thought about Mitch Mitchell since the last shift we'd worked together at Smiley's. I barely knew him, but he was as weird as his name. Supposedly, his mother had pulled him out of some kind of cult in Indiana.

"So he was just sitting there watching me passed out?" I asked.

"I guess," Wexler said.

"Wow. Thanks for your concern, Mitch," I said.

"Can you imagine if you'd gotten away with it?" Wex said. "And then, just when you think you're home free, Mitch Mitchell of all people comes along and blows the whole thing wide open."

"I mean, maybe," I said. "He doesn't really seem like the vindictive type."

"He doesn't seem like any type," Wexler said. "That's the problem. It's always the ones you don't see coming you have to watch out for."

"Well, it's not like you work there anymore," Anna said. "You'll probably never see this guy again, so don't worry about it."

"Still, why would he tell me all that for no reason?" Wex asked.

"Maybe it was just his way of finding something to talk about," Anna said. "I mean, does he even have any friends?"

"Hey, what are you doing?" Wexler asked, suddenly looking off camera at Anna. I could see they were pulling over to the side of the road.

"There's Berylin," she said. "I just need to talk to her for a second."

"I thought you said she was in Myrtle Beach," I said.

"I thought she was," Anna said.

If it was a lie, it was a pretty smooth one. I wondered how

all this might have played out if I'd been home for the summer. They would have had to be more open about it in that case, wouldn't they? Or would Wex have lied about it then, too? Would Anna?

"So what else is going on?" I asked.

"Not much," Wex said. "Same old."

"What are you guys doing tonight?"

"Just hanging out."

"Not going to a movie?" I asked.

It was a dick question, considering I knew the answer, but I felt a little entitled after my conversation with Anna. I wanted to see what he'd say, even if it was like picking at a scab just to get that little stinging feeling.

"Nah. There's nothing to see," he said.

And there it was.

I didn't know how to juggle it all—what I knew, what he thought I knew, how I felt about it, how I might have felt if he hadn't lied—all while having this supposedly normal conversation.

The other relevant fact was, our time together was over anyway. Wex and Anna were both leaving town before I'd even be back to get my stuff and head to Birch. It didn't seem like a scab worth picking—not more than I already had.

"You know what? I actually have to go," I said. "The wedding's coming up this weekend and there's stuff going on here. My dad's waiting for me. Talk to you guys later?"

"For sure," Wex said. "Have a good rest of the night."

"Later," I said.

Just *Later*. Not *You too*. Because, as the very pettiest part of myself seemed to insist just then, they could take care of the rest themselves.

7:48

It was starting to feel like I hadn't completely lost out by coming to California after all. Even from a distance, things were getting uncomfortable between me and Wex. And Anna. But mostly Wex. Not to mention whatever might have happened with that whole Mitch Mitchell thing if I'd stayed home. It wasn't hard to imagine some extreme weirdness on that front, just based on what little I knew about him.

Good luck, dude, I thought, and sent a little packet of good vibes to that still-back-in-Ohio version of myself, for whatever it was worth. Because I had a feeling he just might need it.

11:43

Hey Swift, you awake?	
	Hey. What are you doing?
Nothing. I'm just in a bad mood and sitting here trying to think happy thoughts . . .	
	Like Peter Pan
Huh?	

	In the story. That's how they fly. Pleasant thoughts.
I thought you were talking about peanut butter.	
	Hell no. I'm Skippy all natural, all the way. Peter Pan can suck it.
Ha. Chunky or smooth?	
	Either one
Wrong answer. Chunky. Always.	
	I didn't know you were so rigid
You said rigid :)	
	Don't go there
I'm not sure that's up to me anymore	
	Why? What's happening now?
Pleasant thoughts	
	In that case, keep going

Chapter Nine

9:35

I had a lot to think about that morning. I wished I had Mitch's number. I'd thought about taping a note to his door before I left for the airport, but I didn't want him to see me. The way we left things didn't exactly scream *Please wake me up at the crack of dawn to apologize*.

In the meantime, I had no way of knowing which pieces of my life were collapsing behind me as I flew farther and farther away from the wreckage. It was like I knew a bomb had gone off, but I was still waiting for the body count.

I didn't get to talk to Wex until my layover in Chicago, and even then, there wasn't much to say.

"What do you think I should do?" I asked him.

"I'll find out when Mitch's next shift is. Then I'll try to track him down and talk to him before he goes in," Wex said. "See if he's thinking about doing something stupid."

"Can you just ask him to call me, or to give you his number so I can call him?" I asked. "And tell him that I'm really sorry. I really am, Wex. He didn't deserve that."

"Maybe, but then he shouldn't have started in with you, getting all weird and shit in the first place," Wex said.

Wex was being loyal, which I appreciated, but there was no gray area in my mind about this. I was the one who'd set the whole thing in motion, as soon as I picked up that whipped cream can that night.

The timing sucked, too. It was a quick layover and they were already boarding my flight. A lot could happen in the next five hours; not to mention the next three days.

"Anyway, I'll see what I can do," Wex said. "Try not to worry."

I was definitely going to worry.

"I'll check back as soon as I land," I said. "And thanks. I owe you."

"You don't," he said.

And maybe I didn't. At least, not yet.

11:12

I was starting to feel as though the balance had shifted. Now it seemed like maybe that other version of me, the one in California, had gotten a better summer after all. He had to live with Dad, sure, but he also got to have this imaginary (to me, not to him) boyfriend, which was maybe a net positive, or at least made me stop feeling sorry for him and start feeling envious.

It also hit me somewhere in the air that the two of us

were about to cross theoretical paths for the first time, seeing as how we were both going to the same wedding.

There were, of course, infinite other versions of me, having infinite other experiences, but I wasn't thinking about them. I was thinking about this me. This Chris. The one who was already in California. The one I'd been looking out for, in my own way. And also the one who was falling in love with Swift, I decided, because Anna wasn't the boss of me, so why not? That's the upside of infinite possibilities. Maybe I couldn't control the one I was living, but I could do whatever I wanted with all the rest.

Did he even know that it was me who'd sent Swift his way? Did he think about this stuff like I did? Probably so. He was still me, after all.

And of course—was there anything at all to be gained by wondering about silly shit like this? Yes. No. Maybe. Of course. If nothing else, it made for a decent distraction.

I kept on crafting it in my mind—the summer I was having with Swift. It was like an empty dollhouse of an idea, and I started putting in furniture. Picking out little rugs. Choosing paint colors.

I thought about where we'd go. What we'd do. The first time we'd get naked. How hard it would be for me (for him) to believe he could get that lucky, and how irrefutable it would be, once it was actually happening.

For that matter, I thought, maybe he could do some of the same in return. Maybe he could sit out there in his

reality and send me back some good luck of my own—
especially with Mitch.

Considering how much I was probably going to need it
now, I'd take any help I could get.

5:35

Another five hours, one awkward hug, and ten mostly silent minutes of waiting for my luggage later, Dad and I were
on our way back to his house for the wedding weekend. He
didn't say a word about my nose, which might have been
for my sake, or might have just been him being him. The
first real thing he said, once we were in the car, was—

"Listen, I know this isn't how you want to be here, but
I'm glad to see you."

As if there *were* some way I wanted to be there. Still, I
was less than twenty-four hours post-Mitch, and I'd had
my fill of assholing for a while.

"We don't need to talk about it," I said, which was true.
"It's fine." (Less true.)

I kept checking my phone for messages, as if it wouldn't
chime to let me know when something came in. And even
though I knew Wex would be in touch as soon as there was
something to tell, I couldn't help poking at him one more
time while Dad went on about something I wasn't listening to anyway.

Anything?	

"Chris?"

I looked up.

"Sorry?"

"Did Felicia ask you about taking some video for us at the wedding and reception?" Dad asked.

She had. And I would. I'd brought the Canon they'd given me for graduation, although it was still in the box. But it only seemed polite to use it instead of my phone.

"Yeah," I said.

"Great. Thank you."

"Sure."

"That'll be nice."

"Good."

I kept forgetting—or losing track of the idea—that everyone else who was coming to the wedding thought of it as this champagne-soaked, all-good thing, and entirely worth celebrating. Mark and Felicia, together forever, whatever.

At the same time, there was a little bit of *What the hell is wrong with me?* mixed in there. Seriously, why couldn't I just be neutral about it, or even, god forbid, happy for them? Why did everything always have to be so considered and examined and dissected? By the time you finish dissecting anything, it's a disgusting mess. So what did I expect? That I was going to chew on all this wedding stuff, spit it out, and like what I saw?

Please.

Honestly, what I really wanted—what I'd always wanted with regard to Dad—was to not think about it. But that never seemed like an option. He had this sway over me; this way of invading my thoughts that only got worse when I was around him. Whether that was about my own weak-mindedness, or his strength, or something else, I don't know, but I resented it as much as anything.

It was going to be a long three days.

Chapter 10

6:28

"Okay," Martina told us about halfway through the next meeting, "I have a little activity for you guys."

She got up and started handing out index cards and Sharpies.

"I want you to write down one challenge from this past week. Something that stands out. Just say it in one, two, or three words. And when you're done, go ahead and put the card on the floor where we can all see."

I didn't have to think. I wrote MY FATHER and dropped it on the floor. A minute later, MY FATHER was sitting there alongside Swift's SCHOOL, and everyone else's MOM A BITCH, WANT TO USE, CARLY, GOT HIGH, NEED A JOB, CAR PAYMENTS, MY WIFE, DEPRESSED, FAMILY REUNION, CAROL OD'D, $$$, and THIS IS BULLSHIIIIT.

Then we went around and everyone was supposed to say something about what they'd written. There was an argument (in my head, anyway) that I'd gotten burned the last time and

I should just pass when my turn came. The counterargument was that I should get over myself and participate.

"What about your father?" Martina asked, when it came to me.

"We don't really get along," I said.

"Can you say a little more?"

"Basically, he's an asshole," I told everyone. "Like at the cellular level."

A couple of guys laughed, and not in a bad way.

"I can relate," Tucker said.

"Is that it?" Martina asked.

I thought about it again. "I mean, to be fair, I know it's a two-way street," I said. "But it's like it's contagious or something. Like he makes me that way. I'm a different person around him, and I'm sick of it."

I was also conscious of Swift the whole time, forming whatever opinions he might have been forming. But maybe this was a good thing. I didn't want to waste what little time we'd have together talking about Dad.

"Your father took away any control you had over this part of your life," Martina told me. "So that makes me wonder, how can you *get* more control without doing something you regret?"

"Meaning . . . ?" I asked.

Martina looked around the circle. "Everyone in this room has to learn to cope with triggers. Sometimes it's about *how can I avoid using a given substance?* Other times, that 'substance' is something more like anger, or resentment. And the question is, what's it costing you to keep using it? In other words, what's it costing you to be this person you don't want to be?"

"Okay," I said, taking it in. This stuff was like algebra to me. It made enough sense while I was sitting there in the room, but something told me it was going to lose all its meaning once I was back home, trying to figure it out on my own.

"So I want to give you an assignment," she said.

Speaking of school.

"For the next week, I want you to really think about how you respond to him. And if you can't keep your cool a hundred percent of the time, then just *notice* when he sets you off. Take stock of the fact that it's happening, and why."

That sounded a lot easier said than done, too.

I got what she was saying, though. Dad was *one* of my problems. How I acted around him was another. And the place where those two problems overlapped was the darkest portion of the whole diagram.

Maybe that was why I was here.

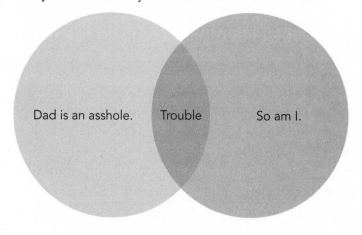

I almost wanted to ask Martina how long she'd been waiting to say this to me. Was it just spontaneous? Or was it more like that subtly bitchy moment at the end of *The Wizard of Oz*, where Glinda tells Dorothy she's had the solution with her the entire time?

Bwitch, why didn't you tell me that back in Munchkinland?

And the answer of course was that Dorothy had to figure it out for herself. We all do, supposedly. But I was still more than a few heel clicks away from home free.

"Yeah, okay," I said. "I can give that a shot." My voice sounded flat and perfunctory, but that was only because I was getting self-conscious. It was like some inaudible timer had gone off and we'd suddenly been talking about me for too long.

Still, I knew what I wanted to do now—how I wanted to use Martina's assignment, and how I wanted to start taking control, at least in the short term.

It was time to start telling the truth.

By which I mean, it was time for Dad to meet Swift.

7:04

"Hey, do you have a second?" I asked Swift as soon as the meeting broke up. "I want you to meet my dad."

"You do?" he asked. He'd heard enough about Dad that it was probably out of left field for him. I hadn't expected this sudden turn myself, but right now seemed like the time.

I nodded. "I'm not going to pretend you don't exist," I told him. "That's what he did to me four years ago."

I was excited now, but also nervous. This was a chance to move off the spot where I'd been stuck since I got to California, and I wanted to do it before I could change my mind.

"Okay then," Swift said. "But come here." He pulled me into a little side hallway and kissed me. "That's for good luck."

A few of the guys saw as they were walking by, but Swift never cared about that, and as far as I could tell, nobody else did, either. So I put my hand in his and walked with him out the front door of Linton Family Services to wait for Dad, who had texted to say he was running late from work.

Of course.

7:19

Dad didn't show any emotion when he pulled up and saw Swift and me standing there, hand in hand. I motioned at him to roll down the passenger window, and he did.

"Dad, this is Swift," I said. My voice wavered more than I wanted it to. I wasn't afraid, but something was making my heart race.

"Hello," Dad said. He was flat. Not rude, not friendly.

"How are you doing?" Swift said. "I've heard a lot about you."

I don't know if Swift realized what a loaded statement

that was. Even Dad could probably guess that he hadn't been getting the world's best reviews from me.

"I know this means you and I have some stuff to talk about," I told Dad. "But I wanted you to know why when I brought it up."

"Okay then," Dad said, in this neutrally ungenerous way. His definition of *stuff to talk about* was going to be different from mine, but I was determined to hold on to the suggestions Martina had made.

Stay calm.

Tell the truth.

Just notice the triggers.

It was a half-hour drive home from where we were. I could maintain anything for thirty minutes, couldn't I?

"Well, we'd better get going," Dad said.

"Nice meeting you," Swift said, and when he turned to say goodbye to me, I was suddenly afraid he might kiss me. I wasn't ready for that. Not in front of Dad.

"I'll talk to you soon," I said. And then he did kind of kiss me, but just with his eyes. They seemed to say *good luck* again, and I tried to answer (*thanks*), whether or not he caught it in the silence. Then I forced myself to open the car door and get inside with Dad.

Here went nothing.

And/or everything.

7:21

We rode for a couple of blocks in silence, playing the *you first* game. I wasn't trying to be stubborn, though. It was more that I hadn't thought this through, beyond introducing Swift to Dad. Now I didn't know what to say.

"So, are you two dating?" he finally asked.

Trigger 1. I breathed through how much I hated that word. I knew what he meant, and that's what mattered, right? Theoretically.

"I guess," I said. "Just hanging out."

"But you told me he wasn't gay," Dad said. "Were you lying? Or did you really think he wasn't?"

"I didn't know at first."

"But you figured it out since then," he said. "Isn't that right?"

Trigger 2. And the ancient pattern resurged. Dad's favorite questions were always the ones that forced you to agree with him.

"I didn't want to get into it," I said. "I was afraid you'd be stubborn about the whole going-out rule. But things have changed, and I wanted to be honest about it now."

"Well, I don't know how I feel about that," Dad said.

Trigger 3. As if that were the only thing that mattered.

"I'm just asking for a little room to go out," I told him. "I don't even have to drive. He has a car."

"So, you want me to trust someone from your *drug group* to drive you around," he said. "Are you even listening to yourself?"

Trigger 4.

"Are *you* listening to me?" I asked before I could stop. Already, I was failing Martina's assignment. And then he answered my question with another question.

"Have you already been out with him?"

I paused. "No."

"What's that pause?"

"Nothing," I said. "We had pizza. On campus. And also after the last meeting." Which I guess from Dad's perspective constituted two more infractions. I could just see it on his face as he added it all up.

"There have been a lot of lies ever since your accident," he said. "If that story about you hadn't shown up in the newspaper, would you have ever owned up to what really happened?"

No. Obviously. I didn't say so at first, but then went with it.

"Probably not, but do you really want to talk about that?" I asked.

"Excuse me?"

"Because in that case, let's talk about the day you left home, and the whole six months before."

"No," Dad said, flat out. "I'm not going to discuss that, least of all right now. Don't change the subject."

"I thought the subject was owning your mistakes," I said. "And lying. And trust."

"Your lies. My trust," Dad said. "How much does Gina know about this?"

— 226 —

"She doesn't have anything to do with it," I said.

"I think she does," he answered.

But I wasn't going to let him sidetrack me. I couldn't even if I wanted to at that point. I was in an emotional riptide now, and I could just imagine Martina, waving at me from the shore while I got pulled farther and farther away.

"I think the only reason you don't hate yourself for what you did to me and Mom four years ago is because you don't even think about it," I said. "You just wrote a letter and disappeared. Do you know you never even apologized to me for that?"

"Hang on—"

"Answer the question!" I shouted at him.

He pulled over then, and stopped in front of a drugstore. When he turned toward me, there was a look in his eyes I hadn't seen before. A different kind of focus, like he was actually looking at me, in a way he never did.

"The world just revolves around you. Is that it? You're the only one that matters? Or ever mattered?" he asked.

I laughed. I wanted to cry, too, but it was too bizarrely funny.

"What in god's name are you smiling at?" Dad asked.

"You have no idea what a hypocrite you are," I said. "How do you think I got this way? Did you ever think maybe all of this"—I passed my hand back and forth between us—"didn't start with me?" It was pouring out now, like a monologue I didn't realize I'd memorized. "You sell yourself as some kind of hero. Some big deal who's important because he believes he's important, not because he actually is. You're just a genius, Dad. That doesn't make you a hero. It never has. It just makes you an asshole."

Dad's hand came up, faster than I would have thought. It was like a starburst. Everything disappeared for a fraction of a second, replaced by the sharp sting of the smack. Then the world refocused as the pain in my cheek reverberated— stronger at first—before it faded in comparison to everything else squirming through my mind.

Dad looked as surprised as I'd felt when he hit me. He was breathing through his nose now, trying to rein himself in. I was shaking, too. I opened the car door and got out.

"Get back here!" he said.

"Go fuck yourself!" I said, loud enough for people on the street to hear. I wanted them to hear. He cared more about strangers' opinions than mine. Which made it a weapon.

As I walked away, he came up fast and grabbed my arm from behind. When I yanked it back, he seemed to re-center himself, and kept his hands at his sides. People were staring. Everything was suddenly loaded in a whole new way.

"Will you please get back in the car?" he asked me. "I'm sorry."

"No," I said. "I've got it from here. And by the way, you can still go fuck yourself, because I quit."

"Chris."

"I'll see you later," I said.

"Chris."

And as I walked away, I could only imagine him standing

there alone on the sidewalk, because if there was one thing I wasn't going to do now, it was look back.

7:26

Hey. You still in the area?	
	Yeah why? What's up?

7:42

"What is it?" Swift asked as soon as I got in his car.

"I'm pretty sure I'm not going to college this fall," I said. "At least not to Birch. And I'm pretty sure I won't be in California much longer, either."

The last part settled like a new weight on my chest. There was nothing I wanted to go home to more than I wanted to stay in California now. Not since Swift. I'd been dragged out here, and now I was going to be dragged back.

"Seriously? What happened?"

I motioned up the street. "Could we just go?"

"Yeah, of course," he said.

I put my foot up on the dash and crammed myself into place as we took off. I felt like I needed to be secured.

"Do you want to talk about it?" he asked, once we were moving.

"I don't even know where to start," I said. "Literally. I don't know what the beginning of all this was."

"Well, you were born," Swift said with a dark smile.

"Right. And then about ten minutes ago, I told Dad to go fuck himself, and I quit my job," I said. "Am I leaving anything out?"

"I guess that covers it."

I reached over and put a hand on his leg. "Thank you for coming to get me," I said.

"Not a problem," he told me. "Close your eyes. Just relax and breathe. I got this."

For a while, neither of us said anything. We rolled down the windows and let the summer air wash over us while Swift drove out of Gisomo Hills and onto the interstate.

"Where are we going?" I asked finally. Not that it mattered.

"To the ocean," he told me.

Of course we were. God, he was good.

"Isn't that like two hours away?" I asked.

"Yeah." He picked up speed as he merged into the highway traffic. We wouldn't get there until at least nine-thirty, and then there was the whole drive back. Swift seemed to assume I could stay out as long as I wanted. At which point, I realized, I could. So I texted Dad.

Not coming home tonight. If you need to be reminded, I'm eighteen. I'll take whatever comes with all that. See you tomorrow. I can pack then if you want.	

The timing was a disaster. I felt bad for Felicia, but maybe it was just as well. They weren't going to want me at the wedding now. Not after this. I wondered if it was too late to get a flight out the next day, and if it made sense for me to try to pay for it myself.

Except, I didn't want to leave. And, I didn't know how not to.

I also didn't know exactly how Dad was going to be about the whole thing. Even for us, this was a new low. But for the time being, with Swift driving me away from it all, it was hard to care. And maybe that was the best possible thing. Not caring for a while sounded ideal.

"Are you thinking about your dad?" he asked. I guess it showed.

"No," I said, only because I didn't want to be. "Not anymore. Starting now." Then I turned off my phone, even if I couldn't do the same for my brain, and tried to enjoy the ride.

9:47

We drove for a while, and talked for a while, and wound up off the interstate, riding along some back road somewhere. Eventually, we picked up the ocean and continued along the coast. There was nothing around but night sky, stars, and water, which just looked like a black infinity bleeding into a black sky.

Swift pulled off at a dirt overlook and cut the engine.

"Where are we?" I asked. I hadn't seen any other cars for miles.

"Near Mendes," he said. It didn't mean anything to me, but I liked that. If I didn't know where I was, that meant nobody else in the world knew, either.

I thought about a map of the United States, and this huge piece of land we were parked on the edge of. In front of me, I had the entire Pacific Ocean, and behind me, its opposite, a whole continent's worth of solid ground, stretching back to Green River, Wex, Anna, and beyond.

Which put us somewhere in the middle, as lost as you could get in two hours and a car. That impossibly empty space in front of me seemed to wipe my mind clean. It was like someone had taken an eraser to the black scribble in the thought bubble over my head.

"I think I just relaxed," I said.

"That's the idea," Swift told me.

I knew something else was going to happen, too. With Swift. I'd known it for most of that drive. And I wanted it to. I was also terrified, but fear had never been so irrelevant.

So I leaned across the seat and kissed him first. I didn't have any goal, other than making sure I didn't wait for him to start. That was important, somehow, even if there was no game plan beyond that.

Swift didn't wait for more, and I didn't want him to. His hands were on me, and then mine were on him, while some small part of my brain told me to not just copy what he did.

The rest of me knew what to do, though. Or maybe it

wasn't that. Maybe it was that I didn't care if I got it wrong. Maybe for once, there were no wrong answers.

"I'm sorry if I don't know what I'm doing," I told him. "It's just that I don't know what I'm doing."

"You're fine," Swift said, and laughed, which made me laugh.

I knew I wanted to keep going, but I wasn't sure where this was headed, or how to turn my thoughts about it into words. Which, as it turns out, is a whole other skill set.

"What about . . ." I felt like a cliché, one of those people on TV who just can't bring themselves to say what they're obviously thinking.

What about condoms?

"I don't have any with me," he said. "But there are still things we can do."

I knew that, too. Mom, and even Zoey, had drilled it into me with a handful of supremely uncomfortable conversations over the years.

And we kept going from there. Clothes came off. Things happened. Not everything, but things I'd never done before, and always wanted to. Things I'd thought about two million times, ever since I started having those kinds of thoughts.

The more it went on, the more I never wanted it to end, and the more I gave into the ridiculous lie I was telling myself that might not have been a lie at all—that I was falling in love with this boy. Because something told me I was.

They say you'll just know. I'm not sure if that's true, but I can say this much. I'd spent my life knowing for a fact that I wasn't in love and never had been. Now, for the first time,

I had the world's best *maybe* flying around inside my head. I also knew that it felt like my life was falling together on the same day it had fallen apart.

And I thought, *Thank you.* Not to Swift, although him too. But to whoever had sent all of this my way.

Thank you.

Thank you.

Thank you.

Chapter Ten

7:28

After he picked me up at the airport, Dad took me straight to the house, mercifully enough. I didn't want to be stuck in the car with him any longer than I had to. I'd say we kept running out of things to talk about, but we never really found anything to run out of in the first place. Which didn't stop Dad from going on about work (= himself), and the wedding, and work (= himself), and Violet, and Dave, and work (= himself), and Zoey. Mostly, I just listened. Nothing new there.

When we got to the house, David and Zoey were sitting around the kitchen table with Felicia and Violet, and what looked like the remains of a huge dinner.

"Heyyyy!" Zoey said, wrapping me up in a big hug. David piled on and hugged the hug, and I saw, between the two of them, that Violet had stood up, fiddling with the hem of her shirt like she didn't know where to put her hands. Or any of herself.

"Hey, Violet, aren't you going to get in on this?" I asked.

Then she smiled, and did. So far, she seemed excited about picking up three new siblings, step or otherwise. And she still got to be the baby. Technically, I was the one giving up that spot.

I wondered for half a second if we were all going to be senior citizens together, doing family Christmases and vacations, or if Dad and Felicia were going to be ancient history by then. The truth is, my money wasn't on this marriage, but that was also exactly the kind of shit I was trying to leave outside.

Felicia kissed me on both cheeks, which was weird, but friendly. "Sit," she said, pushing me into a chair. "Sit, sit."

I left my phone faceup on the table where I could see it. Mostly, I was wondering when Wex was going to be in touch, and what he'd have to say, and what all I'd have to spend the next three days keeping to myself.

David put two hands on my shoulders from behind and squeezed just enough to hurt. "It's good to see you," he said.

"You too," I told him.

"Your nose doesn't look as weird as I thought it would."

"Shut up," I said, but if anyone could get away with that, it was David.

"Does it hurt?" Violet asked.

"Does what hurt?" I asked, and she laughed, and kind of lasered in on me, with both hands flat on the table. It was a little odd, but then, so was her mom. "No," I said. "The truth is, it never really did."

"It barely looks like anything. Just stand a little sideways for the wedding pictures and nobody will ever know," Zoey said, before Felicia stepped in to save me.

"You want something to eat. I know you do," she said. She'd already put a cloth napkin, fork, knife, and a can of Cherry Coke (which she'd remembered I liked), half-poured into a nice glass, over ice in front of me. "Lasagna sound good?"

Much better.

"Lasagna sound amazing," I said.

12:56

Five hours later, we were back at the kitchen table, just Zoey and me this time, staying up late, talking forever, and eating leftovers, like we did.

"So let me ask you," she said. "Did anything else happen the night you had that accident? It seems like there's something you're not saying."

Her voice was low, but it didn't matter. Dad, Felicia, and Violet were all in bed. David was in the TV room.

I squinted at her. I'd decided before I came that I wasn't going to tell Zoey or David what really happened, but I'd also already paused too long for a clean denial.

"What?" she asked.

"Nothing," I said. "I mean—isn't it better if you don't ask?"

Zoey stuck her finger into the bottom of a piece of chocolate cream pie and scooped out the chocolate, leaving the cream and crust behind.

"So obviously there's something," she said. "Just tell me you're being careful. Or at least not completely stupid all the time."

"I'm not being completely stupid," I said.

Not all the time.

"And what about sex?" she asked.

"What about it?"

"Same question. Are you being careful?" she asked. "I mean, you're using condoms, right?"

"Seriously?" I asked.

"Seriously."

When I was little, Zoey would always barge into my room without knocking, and just start talking to me about whatever was on her mind. This was the adult version of that.

"Yes," I said. "I'm using condoms."

And I had, twice, after Mom came home from some meeting and gave me a bunch, and told me to practice with them alone so I'd be ready when the time came (her words).

Basically, Zoey wanted to know that I wasn't committing some kind of sexual suicide out there, which I wasn't. The fact that I hadn't had the opportunity to make that mistake yet wasn't anything she needed to know.

"Are *you* using condoms?" I asked.

"All except one time," she said. "And it freaked me out, so don't do it, okay?"

"Cross my heart."

"Oral sex, too. You can get gonorrhea, herpes, chlamydia—"

"Oh my god. I took health, okay?"

"I'm serious," she said. "And if you haven't used them, or if you slip up one time, that's no reason not to go back to it."

"I just told you I was using them," I said. "Can we be done with this?"

For the record, I'm not a prude. It's not like I couldn't go there with my sister. But she always took it too far, even more than Mom.

"Well, anyway," she said, and pointed to my nose again. "Whatever happened there, or didn't happen, just be glad Dad thinks it didn't."

"I am glad," I said, and then, for the record, "Not that there's anything to tell."

Zoey pulled another finger of chocolate out of that pie and then slid the rest across the table, like a dissected frog for me to finish. Which I would.

"Good call, probably," she said.

I knew that, too.

7:08

Early the next morning, I woke up to a text from Wexler.

	Call me when you're alone.

I was sharing my room with David, so I jumped up and took my phone into the bathroom. A few seconds later, I had him.

"Sorry. Did I wake you up?" Wex asked. "What time is it there?"

"Don't worry about it," I said. "What's going on?"

"Well, listen," he said. "I don't really know how to tell you this, but . . . you're not on the schedule at work for next week."

The air rushed out of me, and my lungs seemed to wither in my chest. There was only one reason people didn't show up on the schedule. I'd just lost my job.

"I don't know what to say," Wex told me. His tone was straight out of a hospital corridor. *I'm sorry, we tried everything we could*.

"Do you know for a fact that I'm fired?" I asked. "Like it's for sure?"

"Sheila wouldn't talk to me about it, but when I asked her point-blank, she just looked at me and didn't deny it," Wex said. "And I still haven't found Mitch. I think he's avoiding me, which he should. I'm going to kick his fucking ass, is what I'm going to do."

"Don't!" I said. "For real. Please."

That was the last thing I needed. Maybe I didn't owe Mitch an apology anymore, but maybe I'd also just gotten what I deserved for what I'd done to him. And besides, I didn't want Wex going out on any limbs for me that I wasn't willing to go out on my own. Kicking anyone's ass just wasn't a concept that applied to me, as much as I wish it did, sometimes.

"Yeah, okay," Wex said. I could just feel him walking himself back. He so badly wanted to do something about this, and I appreciated it.

"How about this?" Wex said. "It's not too late to get him fired, too."

"What do you mean?" I asked.

"Your little surveillance video."

"I erased it," I said. "Two nights ago."

"Yeah, well, I didn't," he said. "I still have the copy you sent me."

"*Oh*," I said, and just sat there for a few seconds, long enough for my mind to cycle through *hmm*, *maybe*, and *no*. "Thanks, but don't do anything with that, either. It's not like that's going to get me my job back."

"So you're just going to let him get away with this?" Wex asked.

"I don't know," I said. "Let's just wait until I get home. If I'm fired, I'm fired. We can still go after Mitch then, if we want to."

I knew I wouldn't want to, but it seemed like an easier way to get to the end of this conversation than ruling it out completely. I had way too many other things to think about now. Like looking for another job with only a month left at home. And figuring out how to keep my parents from finding out what had just gone down.

Because the last thing I needed either of them to know right now was the truth.

Chapter 11

5:55

Swift dropped me off at home just before six. I'd texted Dad to let him know I was okay a few times, but now I had to face him. I hated getting out of Swift's car, especially not knowing if our first night together was also going to be our last.

"Good luck," he said, and waited for me to get to the door before he pulled away.

When I got inside, I found a note taped to the banister. *Please wake me up if I'm asleep when you get here.* I just wanted to go to bed, or maybe start packing, but I went up to Dad and Felicia's room instead, and knocked on the door.

"Dad?"

I heard Felicia say something. Then Dad's voice.

"Come in," he said.

It was still dark, with the shades drawn. Dad was up on his elbows, and Felicia was looking at me with her head still on the pillow.

"Hey, hon," she said. "You okay?"

"I'm okay," I said.

Dad rubbed his eyes, and I thought about how all those people who were fans or admirers of his would never see him like this, all bed-headed and bare shouldered.

"I'll be right down," he said.

I closed the door, went to the kitchen, and chugged an iced coffee. I hadn't slept at all, and the gas station coffee Swift and I had gotten on the way back was useless.

I was standing at the kitchen island when Dad showed up in shorts and a UC T-shirt, scratching his head. My brother and sister were presumably sleeping upstairs. They'd both come in the night before, David from Oregon and Zoey from Michigan, where she'd just graduated. The wedding was a little over twenty-four hours away; thirty to be exact.

"First of all," Dad said, "I'm sorry about yesterday. There's no excuse." He came farther into the room and stood across from me, keeping to his side of the island.

"If you ever hit me like that again, I'm going to hit you back," I said. "Just so you know."

"I'm *never* going to do that again," Dad said. "But fair enough."

I could tell something had shifted. For both of us.

"I'm sorry for the way I went off," I said. I meant in the way I'd spoken to him, not the way I left the car, but I didn't clarify. "And I know the timing sucks. I'm sorry about that, too. But I don't think I was completely wrong, either."

"Maybe not," Dad answered. Even a lukewarm allowance like that was enough to open some slack in the line between us, and I floated free for a few beats, figuring out what to say.

"So what happens now?" I asked.

"Do you still want to go to Birch?" he asked.

"Yeah, but not like this."

"Like what?"

That wasn't such an easy question to answer. Partly because it had so many tentacles.

"I want to keep seeing Swift," I said. "I think I deserve that much."

"Have you done drugs since you've been here?" Dad asked.

"No."

"Do you want to?" he asked.

I'm not sure who he thought I was, relative to all that, but it felt like another box he wanted to put me in.

Trustworthy		Not trustworthy
Non–drug user	No in-between	Drug user
Good son		Bad son

"Not exactly," I said. "But if we're being honest, I'm pretty sure I haven't smoked my last weed, and I'm guessing I'll be drunk more than once before freshman year is over." I heard my own words, and added, "Assuming I get to go."

"I never expected you to abstain from everything under the sun," Dad said. "If that was ever unclear, then I'm sorry."

It was never clear. Which also wasn't worth saying.

"But I don't have to do any of that while I'm here," I said. "For whatever it's worth."

Dad didn't answer. Instead, he went to the fridge and took out some bacon and eggs. "You want?" he asked.

"No thanks."

He started making breakfast, and neither of us said anything for a long time, until he had a pan heating on the stove and a few eggs cracked in a bowl.

"So is this guy your boyfriend?" he asked then. I still didn't know what that word meant to him, but—

"I think so," I said.

"Then I imagine you really wouldn't want to leave," he said, and started whisking the eggs. My first reaction was to think something snarky about Dad having an actual human insight, but I stifled that, too.

"Yeah," I said. "I don't want to go."

"I don't want you to, either," he said, which surprised me; not that he'd think it, but that he'd say it out loud. "And I'm glad you have someone."

This was all foreign soil for us, and I felt a little disoriented. "Um, thanks," I said.

Felicia came into the kitchen tentatively, in her bathrobe, as I kept talking.

"I just want to say for the record, I don't blame anyone but myself for what happened that night at the restaurant. And I'm going to try to not be such a jerk all the time from now on."

Dad and Felicia looked at each other. I obviously wasn't the only one a little surprised by this whole conversation.

"I just need to know that you have the capacity to think these things through," Dad said. "And even if you make mistakes, that they're based on some grounding in intelligent thought."

Intelligent thought.

I knew what he meant, but I don't think he knew how insulting that was. "I know what you're trying to say," I told him.

"I'm not *trying*, I'm just—" Dad started, but Felicia put a hand on his arm, and he stopped.

I started again. "I know what you're trying to say, and even though I know it was a dumbass thing to do that night behind the restaurant, it sucks that you doubt me this much."

"I don't *know* you," Dad said. "I barely get to see you, and even when you're here, I just get this husk of a kid."

"I'm not a kid."

He took an openly impatient breath. "You have been up to now," he said. "But it's clear to me that you have a whole other side, or sides, that I don't know about."

He wasn't wrong about that, either, but he also wasn't trying to see beyond the obvious.

"It's not like I'm withholding some secret, put-together version of myself," I said. "I'm trying to figure shit out all the time."

"We know you're doing your best," Felicia said.

"No!" I said, with more force than I meant to. "I'm not. That's what I'm trying to say. I could tell you all kinds of ways I'm not doing my best. I'm not even close."

"Don't be too hard on yourself," Dad said. But even that was nearly impossible to hear, when I'd wanted him to be so much—*so* much—harder on himself than he'd ever been.

And maybe it made sense to just leave it at that. I probably should have, but it also felt like we'd already cracked the patient's chest. If there was anything else to do in there, now was the time.

"Listen," I said. "I have to ask you something else. And don't get mad." Dad dropped three pieces of bacon into the frying pan, and it started to sizzle. "Actually, I'll have some of that," I said, and he put in three more.

I realized suddenly that he never cooked. Not since Felicia. The whole breakfast thing was some kind of protective gear, wasn't it? He had to look at the eggs, the bacon, the pan, not at me. Which was fine. I think it made it easier for both of us.

"Why did you leave the way you did?" I asked.

"What?"

"When you left," I said, "what was that letter all about? You literally never said goodbye."

Dad stopped. Maybe even froze. I couldn't tell what he was thinking.

"How about if we tackle that one another time?" he asked.

"Seriously?"

Even now, I couldn't believe he was going to shut me down like that. But it was as far as we got before Zoey and Violet came in, and Zoey was hugging me hello, and the day before the wedding was officially getting started.

So I guess we'd resolved the battle, if not the war. I could walk away, and keep Swift, and Birch, and let the rest of it go. Maybe for good. Or, I could take this moment, which might or might not come again, and press Dad for an answer to the one thing I'd always wanted to know.

Dad was looking at me like he knew exactly what I was thinking. I stared back, trying to see myself in his face. But I wasn't anywhere in there. I looked like Mom, except for my nose, now.

"Hey, is it too late for a couple of eggs?" I asked.

"Not at all," Dad said, gratefully, if I'm not mistaken. "How do you want them?"

7:19

Guess who's not going anywhere?	
	You'd better mean you or I'm going to be really disappointed
Surprise	
	Awesome awesome awesome. When can you hang again?
Now, I wish. Soon though. I have a lot to tell you about.	

9:31

After breakfast, I went up and said hi to David, who was still in bed. Zoey trailed in behind me, and the three of us got down pretty quickly to talking about everything that had happened.

"You complain about him a lot. You know that, right?" David asked.

David was a lot of fun, and hilarious most of the time, but he was also a pain in the ass.

"Is that a real question?" I asked. "Or more like a Dad question?"

"Meaning what?" he asked.

"Meaning, when was the last time you had to live and work with him twenty-four seven? Never, that's when."

"Dave and I lived with him all the way through high school," Zoey said. "You got rid of him in eighth grade, so . . ."

"Speak for yourself," David said to Zoey. "Don't lump me in with the suffering masses."

"Here we go," I said.

"Unlike you two, I don't feel the need to constantly bitch about my past," he said. He was sitting up now, drinking the coffee I'd brought him, and picking up steam. "It's a waste of time. It's a waste of *life*."

Zoey went over and put a hand under his chin. "Who forgot to hold you when you were a baby?" she asked. It was an inside joke, and about the two hundredth time one of us had used it.

"Do you actually like him?" I asked David. "As a person?"

"Don't be an idiot," he said, which was basically a *no* without having to own it.

"Anyway," I said. "My point is, we worked it out. And I'm not going to shit all over the wedding, if that's what you're wondering."

"No, you already did that," David said.

Zoey flopped down on the single bed next to me and made me scoot over. "Don't ruin this for them," she said.

"I just said I wasn't going to," I told her. "Why did you hear the opposite of that?"

"It's not the opposite. I mean you're here, but are you *here*?" she asked. "I don't think it's fair to sit through a wedding all uptight, especially after running off, or whatever it was you were doing last night. I'm not judging. I'm just saying."

"I'm judging," David said. "You're being a little asshole. Just let this weekend be about them. How about that?"

"It is," I said. "I mean, it will be. It's all taken care of. Dad and I talked it out. It's behind us now."

"Thank god," David said.

"Yeah, right," Zoey said.

Chapter Eleven

12:52

I was running out of reasons for not calling Smiley's. I just wanted to know for sure if I needed to be thinking about finding another job. It was already late July and I was going to need all the jump on this I could get.

So while the tent people were putting up a tent in the backyard for the wedding, and Felicia was cooking like crazy, and Dad was at work, and Zoey, Violet, and Dave were out running errands, I went to the upstairs bathroom, closed the door, and called the restaurant.

I don't know why I'd been thinking it was a bad idea to ask Sheila about it point-blank. The worst she could do was not take my call.

But she took it.

"I'm kind of surprised to hear from you," she said. That seemed like a bad sign, although she also sounded sympathetic, for whatever that was worth.

"So, just to be clear," I said. "I'm fired, right?"

"Well . . . *yeah*," she said, like it was the least necessary question possible.

"Are you allowed to tell me what Mitch said?" I asked.

"About what?" she asked.

About what?

That seemed weird. I took a beat before I said anything else, but I could already tell that something was off.

"Did Mitch talk to you?" I asked.

"No," she said slowly. Her tone had turned suspicious. "Why? Is there something else I need to hear about here?"

Actually, it seemed like there was something else *I* needed to hear about here.

"Well, this may be a weird question," I said, "but why exactly was I fired?"

"What do you know?" she asked.

The balls were flying faster than I could catch them. I forced myself to keep going slowly.

"All I know is that I'm not on the schedule for next week," I said. "But that's it. Please, Sheila? Just tell me. I'm kind of freaking out here."

There was a pause. I heard a door close before she went on, and I could just imagine her huddled there in that tiny cube of an office, bent over the phone.

"Chris, you told the ER doctor yourself what happened on the night of your accident," she said. "That's not something an insurance company is going to miss."

"Oh," I said.

Holy.

Shit.

"That."

"I'm really sorry about how all this went down," Sheila said. "I mean, obviously it's your fault, but there is one other thing you should know."

"Oh, god."

"Actually, it's good news," she said.

I couldn't even imagine how that might be the case.

"They're going to fulfill the worker's comp claim anyway."

"Seriously?" I asked. "Why? I mean . . . how? I mean—" I didn't know what I meant.

"That adjuster who interviewed you? I guess she had some kind of family situation, and I guess the guy who was supposed to take over her files just switched offices, or email, or something. I'm really not sure, but the deadline for denying the claim came and went yesterday, so they have to honor it. Meanwhile, though, all the information's right there, which is why I have to let you go."

There was another long silence, where I was presumably supposed to say something, but nothing came to mind.

"I think the restaurant just wants this one to go away," Sheila said.

"Wow," I got out. I didn't know what I was going to tell my parents about getting fired, but at least I knew what I wasn't going to say. What I wouldn't have to say, now.

At least that. And that was a lot.

"You're damn lucky. You know that, right?" Sheila asked. "Someone must be looking out for you."

I glanced in the mirror and saw myself looking back, and shook my head at that guy, like *can you believe this?*

Neither of us could.

"Yeah," I said. "Maybe someone is."

1:00

I called Wex right away.

"What's up?" he asked.

"A lot," I said. "But most of all, don't talk to Mitch, okay? Just let it go."

"Too late," Wex said. "I just talked to him."

He had to be kidding me. But, of course, he wasn't.

"How long ago?"

"Like fifteen minutes. I was about to call you."

In other words, if I hadn't put off asking Sheila about this, I could have caught Wexler in time.

"What'd you say to him?" I asked.

"Don't kill me," Wex said.

I sat down on the toilet seat and braced myself for whatever this was about to be.

"Why? What's going on?"

"You're going to kill me," he said.

"Okay, stop saying that and just tell me," I said.

Wexler groaned. "Mitch saw the video," he said.

"What?" I asked. "How?"

"I, um . . ." It was coming out slowly. Reluctantly. "I showed it to him."

"Why would you do that?" I said, louder than I meant to. Zoey, Dave, and Violet were back—I could hear them moving around the house while I was trying not to get too mad, too fast.

"You're not here, man. It's been crazy," Wexler said. "I did try talking to Mitch, and he completely went off on me. It was all 'get out of my face,' and 'you don't know me,' and shit like that. I just had to shut him up. It was either that or knock him down."

I shut my eyes and tilted my head back. There were so many things this meant.

"Wex."

"What?"

"He didn't talk to Sheila. I just got off the phone with her."

"*What?*"

"Yeah. He's not the one who got me fired."

"What happened?" he asked.

"I have to go," I said. And I didn't mean because of everything else happening in the house. It was more about everything I didn't want to say right now.

"What are you going to—" Wexler started to ask.

"Bye," I said, and clicked out.

I sat there, not quite hyperventilating, on the toilet seat. I couldn't believe I'd just hung up on Wex, but I also couldn't believe this had happened. I'd just spent the past ten minutes getting slapped around by good and bad luck in such rapid succession, I didn't know what to think.

Meanwhile, the gap between how big this problem had just gotten and how little I could do about it for the next two days was impossible. My mind was at capacity, and it wasn't going to be emptying out anytime soon.

But hey, at least I didn't have to get dressed up and see my grandmother, aunt, uncle, cousins, and a bunch of people I didn't know for a big weekend full of wedding stuff on top of everything else.

Oh, wait. Yes I did.

Chapter 12

12:34

In terms of clothing and personal hygiene, I tend to play along at the basic membership level. I care what I look like, but at the same time, whenever I see one of those stranded-on-an-island movies, part of me thinks, *Well, at least I wouldn't have to shower.*

So it wasn't like I minded getting dressed for the wedding so much, I just would have minded less in shorts and a T-shirt.

By the time the actual ceremony rolled around, it felt like Dad and I had finally set aside some of our stuff, or at least put it in storage. It was weird to imagine how close everything had come to changing all over again. I could have just as easily been on a plane home to Ohio, with no more Swift and no more Birch in my future. But instead, here I was.

I'd been sending Swift little updates all morning, mostly because it was as close as I could get to having my hands on him, and I couldn't wait for lunch on Monday.

Meanwhile, the backyard looked beautiful. It was all very Felicia, like something out of a magazine, in a good way. There was a high-peaked white tent, with Chinese lanterns hung inside, and jars of wildflowers everywhere, and a little arbor made out of branches painted white for the ceremony.

I sat in front with my grandmother and Zoey, filming from my seat while David and Violet stood up with Dad and Felicia for the vows. I'd been curious about what it would be like to see Dad tackle all those soft, unquantifiable emotions in front of everyone. It seemed pretty incongruous for him, so I guess I shouldn't have been surprised when he started his part with something straight out of academia.

"It was in 1927 that Niels Bohr first introduced the concept of complementarity to the world of science," he said.

And all I could do was smile. It was just Dad being Dad. I was a little embarrassed for him. He didn't even know how he came across sometimes, but I also couldn't ignore the fact that he seemed so obviously happy.

"Complementarity holds that two seemingly incompatible facts can be simultaneously true," he went on. "So for instance, in this universe, Felicia, you are a gorgeous, caring, intelligent, well-spoken, thoughtful woman. And in this very same universe, you are also batshit crazy for marrying a nutjob like me."

He got a big laugh on that one, and then said some more about complementarity, and life in general, while everyone ate it right up. In fact, he was killing it, which was something

I'd never seen before. Not like this. I'd seen him give interviews and lectures, and even sign autographs, but I'd never watched him hold a crowd just as himself.

"The good news in all of it," he went on, "is that both of those truths lead to the same outcome, which is this wedding." Some people actually let out an audible *awww* at that. "And I couldn't be happier to be standing right here, right now, and I don't think I could love you any more than I already do, my beautiful Felicia. But then again, you'll have to ask me about that tomorrow, and the day after, and for every one of our days to come, however many that may be."

Everyone had gone really still by then, except you could hear a few people sniffling. And the weirdest part of all was my own reaction to the whole thing.

"Are you crying?" Zoey whispered. "I'm shocked."

I mouthed a *shhh* and chinned at the camera. I didn't want her to mess up the video, so she just put her head on my shoulder, which made me feel even gushier inside.

I don't know why I had tears in my eyes. It just came over me—the emotion, yes, but also this kind of revelation that Dad and Felicia were in love, for real. Actual love. That's a huge *duh*, I know. It's not like I was unaware of that fact. More like I'd suddenly bothered to notice it. Whatever happened after this, or however long their marriage lasted—or didn't last—the point was that right now, they were going to love each other no matter what.

There was something pure and beautiful about that. Because for all of my cynical buildup to this day, I realized, it didn't matter what I thought, and it didn't matter what I did. I could throw down all the mental roadblocks I liked, and it wouldn't mean a thing to Dad and Felicia, or their happiness. Just to my own, really.

Duh.

Chapter Twelve

12:34

During Dad and Felicia's wedding ceremony, I sat up front with my grandmother and Zoey, filming from my seat while David and Violet stood up with Dad and Felicia for the vows. This was the part I was most curious about—what it would be like to see Dad saying wedding-vow-type stuff in front of all his friends and family, as opposed to hiding behind the whole Professor Schweitzer-PhD-author-genius thing. I'd even said to Zoey earlier, "Watch, he'll just turn this into some kind of lecture."

So when Dad started in with:

"It was Neils Bohr who first suggested the concept of complementarity to the world of science, back in 1927—"

I couldn't help it. I laughed out loud. I really didn't mean to. It just came out, big enough that if it had been a fart, it would have been a top one or two most embarrassing moments of my life. So it wasn't fart bad. But it was bad. Everyone noticed.

Dad turned around and gave me this open look that said, *Seriously?*, which got a laugh of its own from everyone else. Then he turned back to Felicia while I sat there with my face quietly on fire, and the moment, for them, was saved. I couldn't even look at Zoey. I just tried to focus and get as steady a shot as I could.

"As I was saying," Dad continued, to another laugh, and then went right back into embarrassing himself. The more he spoke, the clearer it was to me that we weren't wedding guests at all. We were just receptacles for more of Professor Schweitzer's pearls of wisdom.

For a while, he went on about complementarity, which I knew was a favorite corner of theoretical physics for him. It's all about how, for instance, light can be a particle *or* a wave but not both at any given moment, depending on how you observe it. Or like those figure ground studies, including the one he put on the cover of his book (Was he actually plugging his own book during his wedding?), where it's two faces and a vase, but only one at a time, depending on where you put your focus.

Eventually, Dad flipped the whole thing around and got another big laugh talking about how brilliant and crazy Felicia was at the same time, just for marrying him.

And then, finally, he wrapped up.

"So let me just say, Felicia, that I couldn't feel luckier to be standing here with you, right now, and I couldn't love you any more than I already do," he said. "Although, ask me about that again tomorrow, and the day after, and, if you'll have me, for all of our days to come, however many they may be."

People were sniffling and all, but I just couldn't go there. As far as I was concerned, the whole thing was nothing more than a performance disguised as a human experience.

Not that it mattered what I thought.

That last fact hit me all at once. It was like some headline floating in from an adjacent dimension. *This just in. It doesn't matter what you think of him—especially to him.* Dad and Felicia were going to love each other and be happy whether I saw through him or not.

So maybe I was wasting my own energy. Maybe I could afford to relax once and for all, and just drop all the stupid judgments. In fact, I definitely could. For sure. Yes. Soon.

Just maybe not today.

Chapter 13

1:31

I mostly hung out behind my camera at the reception, taking shots of the party and gathering everyone's messages for Dad and Felicia. It wasn't a bad job to have; definitely better than standing around, not knowing how to be.

They had a big lunch spread, and a little jazz combo so people could eat and then dance it off by the pool. The day was kind of perfect, from what I imagined would be Dad and Felicia's perspective. Even the weather was just right.

All of which was relatively predictable, until I got around to Violet.

"Hey, Violet!" I said, with the camera running, "What do you want to say to Mark and Felicia?"

She smiled self-consciously up from her seat. "Um . . . well, congratulations, you guys, and um . . . welcome to the family. I mean, I know that goes both ways, but . . ." Then she stopped and made a face. "Can we start over?"

I hit Stop. "No problem."

"And can I ask you something first?" she asked before I could restart.

"Sure." I sat down and took a rumaki off her plate and popped it in my mouth. "What's up?"

"What happened with you and Mark the other night?" she asked.

"Oh, that."

There were people all around, but the music was enough of a buffer to put us in our own little bubble right there at the table. In any case, I figured Violet deserved to know, given that she'd been living with it for the past month. So I started by telling her about Swift, mostly just to get to the part about my fight with Dad.

Violet didn't flinch at any of it. She just listened all the way through.

Then she asked, "Why do you hate him so much?"

It made me a little sad that she thought I did. Even if I did. Or had. Or maybe still did, a little.

"It's complicated," I said. "Let's just say I didn't like the way he ended things with Mom. Or with me." There was more I could say, about Dad as a person, but I didn't want to start giving Violet some list of personality flaws to look out for. She still had to live with him for the next four years.

"What do you mean *he* ended things?" she asked.

"What do *you* mean?" I asked. "Do you really need me to spell it out?" I leaned in closer and spoke low but clearly. "My dad had an affair with your mom while he was still married to my mom."

"That's not what happened," she said.

— 266 —

"Oh, because you know."

Violet shrugged but didn't break eye contact. I knew that look. I'd been a little brother all my life, and I knew the rare pleasure of being both the youngest and irrefutably right about something at the same time.

"Everyone around here treats me like I'm invisible," she said. "But guess what? Sometimes invisible people hear things they're not supposed to hear."

After four years of knowing her, Violet was suddenly way more interesting than she'd ever been. "Hang on," I said. "What exactly did you hear?"

The band finished one song and went right into another; something slow that I didn't recognize. Dad took Felicia out onto the little dance floor and pulled her in close while everyone watched.

Violet leaned close, too. "There was some guy named Virgil," she said. "I remember because it was a V-i name, like mine. I guess he and your mom were . . ." She trailed off then and made a *you know* kind of face.

I was still stuck on the name.

"Are you talking about Virgil Auerbach?" I asked.

"I don't know," she said.

Mr. Auerbach had been the principal at the elementary school I went to, and where Mom had taught third grade before she gave it up to start her real estate agency. I didn't even know he and Mom were friends, much less . . . *you know.*

I wasn't sure which part of it bothered me the most, but before I was going to get too worked up about any of it, I needed verification.

"I'll be back," I told Violet, and got up.

"Don't you want to do the video?" she asked, but I was already headed straight for Zoey, where she was standing by the buffet with a glass of champagne.

"Violet just told me something really weird," I said. I turned my back to the rest of the party. "Did Mom have an affair with Mr. Auerbach when Dad was with Felicia?"

Zoey looked at me, blinking. She put two fingers up to her forehead and a thumb on her temple, trying to be funny but also to show me what she thought of the question.

"How about if we have this conversation . . . oh, I don't know . . . *any* other time but right now?" she asked.

In other words—yes. Violet was right.

"So . . ." I'd started to speak before I could put it together, but then, just as fast, got myself the rest of the way there. "Am I the only one who didn't know about this? Literally, the only one?"

Zoey did a slow-motion shrug and shoved a cream puff in her mouth, then garbled out something with hand gestures to the effect of *I can't talk right now, I have a mouth full of cream puff.*

"Just tell me," I said. "I'm serious."

Still, she took her time swallowing and having another swig of champagne.

"You weren't supposed to know about any of it, including Felicia, until after the divorce," she said. "But you already hated Dad, so—"

"Who cheated first?" I asked.

"I don't know," she said dismissively. "Does it matter?"

Did it?

"They stopped loving each other a long time ago," Zoey said. "That much, I thought you knew."

"Did Mom know Dad was leaving?" I asked. I'd always assumed she hadn't.

"No."

"Well, at least I was right about that."

"They knew you were going to want to live with Mom," Zoey said. "I mean, why *would* they tell you? You were only fourteen."

"So is Violet," I said.

Zoey did a mini–double take in Violet's direction. Then she tilted her glass, like she was toasting her from across the tent while Violet stared back, looking confused.

"Girl's got game. I'll give her that much," Zoey said.

And while it was true that everyone knew now, I was the only one who still had to get his head around it. In other words, the party was going great, Dad and Felicia were having a good time, the food was amazing, of course, and everything I'd thought about my father—literally every thought I'd bothered to have about him in the past four years—was built on half a lie. Or half a truth, depending on how you looked at it. I mean, he was still an asshole, after all.

Same guy, different story.

2:11

I wouldn't have thought everything could just go on the way it had been—and yet, everything has a way doing exactly that when you least expect it.

I talked to Swift from up in my room and told him about what had happened. I ate a bunch of really good food. Snuck a glass of champagne.

And eventually got up my nerve to go talk to Gina. I'd seen her across the yard a few times, and during the ceremony, of course, but hadn't figured out what I wanted to say that I hadn't already said. Maybe the whole Mom-and-Dad revelation had put the rest in perspective. Or maybe that little bit of champagne had.

Or both.

"Hey, Gina," I said. She was standing by herself on the back patio outside the kitchen, drinking what I assumed was a Diet Coke, and looking out over the rest of the party.

"Hey, you," she said, neutrally friendly. A little like we barely knew each other.

And I went for it. "Do you want to dance?"

She retracted her head a little, like a turtle, blinking back at me just for a second. But nothing ever seemed to trip Gina up for very long.

"Sure," she said. "Why not?"

We walked over to the little dance floor, where everyone else was doing whatever you do to a jazz combo, which mostly meant touching while they danced. I put up my hand and Gina put hers in mine. I put my other hand on her side, and she did the same. It was super old-school, and not as awkward as it might sound, although I'd say it still qualified as weird. I don't know if I'd ever actually touched Gina before.

Then we started moving. Each of us was as bad a dancer as the other. If there weren't so many physics people there, we might have stood out, but that crowd's not exactly known for their moves.

"Listen, I know I already said this," I told her, "but I'm sorry."

"Don't worry about it," she said. She rolled her head to look at the cloudless sky, and the party around us. "It's a fabulous day. Let's be happy."

"Deal," I said, and we kept dancing. I was glad to clear the air, and to get at least some sense that Gina and I could still be friends. Assuming that's what we'd been. I'd never known anyone like her, so it was hard to gauge.

"Can I ask you something else?" I asked then.

"I think you should stop asking people if you can ask them questions, and just ask the questions," she said.

"Do you love me?"

That stopped her.

"I mean," I said, "do you have to?" We were just standing there now, on the edge of the dance floor. "Is it one of the rules, or whatever? Loving everyone?"

Gina thought about it for a second. "I'd like to *say* that I love everyone," she said. "But it's not always that easy."

I pointed at myself. "Exhibit A," I said, and she smiled back.

"But yeah," she said. "If I speak from my truest heart, on

a good day, I'd say yes. I do love you. And your father. And your family, for that matter."

"Oh," I said. I was mostly at a loss.

She leaned in then, and winked at me. "I also *like* you," she said. "And that part's not required."

"Well, thanks," I told her. "I like you, too." And since I wasn't allowed to ask permission anymore, I moved on to the next question. "Do you want to have lunch sometime this week? Maybe with Swift if he can make it?"

The music was still going, and suddenly, we were dancing again. Such as it was.

"Yeah," she said. "That sounds nice."

Chapter Thirteen

2:30

Even with all the open questions back in Ohio, I didn't answer any of Wex's messages during the reception. I couldn't yet. I really just wanted to wait until I was home again, and start sorting it out then. The damage was done. I'd lost my job. I'd figure out Mitch and Wex and Anna when I could—and when I had to.

I kept my camera going almost nonstop during the party, just to put my mind on something else. I went from the tent to the pool to the house and back again, doing virtual laps and catching as many people as I could.

When I went inside to change batteries at one point, Felicia was in the kitchen, fussing with the food in her nice dress.

"Do you need some help?" I asked.

"Oh, thanks, hon, but I'm good," she said. "You just keep doing what you're doing. I can't *wait* to see it all."

"Okay, then," I said, just as a woman I didn't recognize came in from outside.

"Felicia, put me to work! You should be out there having a good time," she said. She had dark hair and bright-red lips—or lipstick, anyway. It was the thing you couldn't help noticing about her.

"I'm on my way outside right now," Felicia said. "But you're sweet. Hey, Chris, do you know Gina from your dad's office?"

"I don't," I said, and shook her hand.

She flashed me a big smile. "Chris, hi," she said. "It's nice to put a face to the name. Your dad has told me so much about you."

That made sense. A lot of the people who worked with Dad would know something about me. I knew nothing about her, though.

"What do you do at the lab?" I asked.

"Oh, *pfft*, I'm just a drone," she said. "But what about you? I understand you're going to be a film major at college this fall. That's exciting."

"Film and English, double major," I said. Of course Dad had gotten it wrong. "And actually, speaking of film, can I do a little video of you?"

"You want to film me?" she asked.

I held up my camera. "Just a quick message for Dad and Felicia, whatever you want to say. You don't have to, though."

"No, no, it's fine," she said, and followed me outside to the patio, where I could get a nicer shot of the party behind her.

She took a minute to put a fresh, undetectable coat of red over the color already on her lips, then turned to me and bared her teeth.

"All good?" she asked.

"All good," I said, and tried not to laugh, but only because I liked how unselfconscious she seemed. Then I pointed the camera at her and started shooting. "Whenever you're ready."

"Okay, well, hi, Mark and Felicia," she said. "I just want to say congratulations, and thank you for including me in your celebration. God has really smiled down on us with this beautiful day, and I hope it's just the first of many beautiful occasions still to come. Jesus loves you, and so do I. Here's wishing you nothing but the best."

She smiled, super bright, again, and held it, waiting for me to turn off the camera.

"That's great, thanks," I said. I hadn't been expecting the religious stuff, and I was a little afraid she might start asking me if I knew Jesus was my savior or something like that, so I thumbed over at the rest of the party instead. "I'd better keep moving," I told her. "I need to catch as many people as I can while they're here. But it was nice meeting you, Gina."

"You too, and *good luck* in the fall!" she said, just before I moved on and made my escape.

She seemed nice enough, anyway.

3:55

Just as things were starting to wind down that afternoon, I got a call from Anna. When I saw her name on the screen, I wasn't sure whether to pick up or not. It rang three times before I decided.

"Hey," I answered, and walked around the side of the house for a little privacy.

"How's it going?" she asked. I think we both knew that's not why she was calling, though.

"Not great," I said. I wasn't sure if she'd think I was talking about the wedding, or about everything still waiting for me back in Ohio, but I didn't clarify.

"Listen," she said. "Wex is really sorry about what happened. He told me you're not returning his messages."

"I just need to get it sorted out in my head," I said. "I am pissed, but it's not just about one thing."

"What do you mean?" she asked.

"Can we talk about this when I see you?"

"Just tell me the subject, at least," she pressed.

Okay, I thought. *Fine*. I'd give her the headline, anyway.

"The truth is, I was pretty bummed that you guys didn't want to spend that last night with me before I left. That's why I was upset outside Eddie's house. It's been weird for a while, to be honest. It just has."

"I'm so sorry," she said. "This is exactly what I was afraid was going to happen. Though I did ask you to talk to us if it got weird for you. Remember?"

"I know," I said. "But sometimes that's a little like

saying, 'If you break your leg, I want you to run right over here and tell me about it.' It's just not that easy."

"We'll try to do better," she said. "I promise."

I felt guilty for mentioning it now, and I felt guilty for getting some of what I wanted from her, even if I did want it. All I could say was "Thanks. I'll see you the day after tomorrow."

"Call him," Anna said.

"I will. Soon," I said, but I knew I probably wouldn't.

Talk about déjà vu.

Chapter 14

12:12

With everything that happened over the weekend, it felt strange to be back at work Monday morning. Dad and Felicia were going to have some kind of honeymoon that fall, after I'd gone to Birch, and just before Dad started a new sabbatical, which he said was for research on his next book.

Grandma, David, and Zoey had all flown out on Sunday, so the reset factor was complete, like the wedding had never happened at all.

The best part of the day was meeting Swift on the green in front of Moore Hall, without having to trek across campus to stay off Dad's radar. I brought drinks from the lab and tacos from one of the food trucks for both of us. He brought a box of doughnuts from the good place, with three different kinds of cinnamon—powdered, roll, and crumb—because yes, he was that good.

Now we were just sucking up some California sun and enjoying the day.

"So you've seen the ocean," he said. "What do you want to do next?"

"Please tell me you like movies," I said. "I've been going through withdrawal."

Swift rolled onto his back and used my knee for a pillow. "Is there anything good out?"

I smiled down at him. It was the middle of summer. Anyone who can't find a good movie to see in July isn't even trying. "I have so much to teach you," I said.

"Bring it," he said.

"But you're still going to have to pick me up."

"Not a problem."

I had two more meetings to go before I crossed that nonnegotiable finish line, with Dad's car keys hanging just on the other side. His compromise was letting me go out at all. Which I'd take. So now it was just a question of how Swift and I wanted to spend the time we had until I left for college.

And maybe it wouldn't just be a month, either. Maybe I'd be back to see him at Christmas, or on spring break, or all of next summer.

Or maybe this wasn't going to last that long.

Or it would. Spectacularly, for the rest of my life.

Or for a year.

Before it ended badly.

Or sweetly.

Or suddenly.

Or not at all.

But in the meantime, my lunch hour was almost up and I

had to go back to work soon. So I leaned down and gave him a kiss, like a pre-goodbye.

"I can't believe you're going to be gone in a month," Swift said, a little like reading my mind. "That's going to suck."

"Yeah, it is," I said. "But I'm here now, right?"

"That's right," he said. "You, me, doughnuts, and everything."

"In approximately that order," I said.

Chapter Fourteen

3:30

I got home late Sunday night, and didn't go anywhere until just before three-thirty on Monday. I spent the day unpacking, doing laundry, and waiting to head over to Smiley's at the right time.

I knew Mitch worked Monday nights, because that had usually been my shift, too. And I wanted to hand in my uniform, get my last check, and be back outside before he got there.

Which is what happened. I was in my car when he pulled in. And as he got out, so did I.

He looked over at me, paused, and then kept moving. I had to hustle to catch him before he went inside through the back door.

"Can I talk to you?" I asked. "Please?"

Mitch turned his head to the side, like he didn't want to even look at me. But then he pivoted and stared me in the eye after all. I had to fight not to look away.

Go ahead, he seemed to be saying.

"Listen, I just want to start by telling you how sorry I am," I said. "It's true that I didn't trust you, and I really messed up because of that. I don't expect you to forgive me, or to make nice, or whatever. I just need you to know that I know what a huge mistake I made. You didn't deserve any of it, and I'm sorry, which I know means nothing. But I really am."

Mitch spit on the pavement. "I'm so fucking tired of people treating me like shit in this town," he said. "Nobody here even knows me." It was already more than I'd expected him to say. Then he added, "You sure as hell don't."

"Yeah, I learned that," I said. It seemed pretty obvious now, looking back. "Anyway, I'll leave you alone. I mean, unless there's anything I can do. Seriously, anything at all. You could even hit me if you wanted to, and I wouldn't blame you."

I didn't actually expect him to respond to any of that. Much less so fast.

My nose took his fist, hard. It felt like a knife to my sinuses, then an explosion through my head, and a gush out my nostrils. I stumbled back but managed to stay on my feet.

My very first thought was *ARE YOU KIDDING ME?* I was maybe ten steps away from where I'd passed out the night this all began.

But my second thought blocked out the first. *HE'S GOING TO HIT ME AGAIN.*

I put up one hand to shield my nose and held out the other. "Don't!" I said. When I looked up, a rope of blood and snot poured out of me. Mitch was just standing there, staring back. He looked pissed, but also calm.

"Can you get me a paper towel or something?" I asked. My voice was thick with whatever combination of fluids was clogging my throat. I turned away and snot-rocketed whatever I could get out, which was a mistake. It felt like skull fire.

Then I heard a car door slam, and Wex's voice.

"What do you think you're doing?" He was there now, and threw Mitch up against the back door. "You fucking loser!"

"Get off him!" I said. Mitch's hands were still at his sides. He wasn't even trying to fight. I grabbed the back of Wex's uniform and yanked him off. Wex started toward Mitch again, but I put my hands out and got in the way.

"No!" I shouted at him. "Don't! Don't even think about it!" My upper lip was a snotty mess—I knew that without even knowing what else I looked like.

I heard another door slam then, and when I turned around, Mitch had gone inside. Which was just as well. I think we'd both said our piece.

"What's the matter with you?" Wex asked.

"What's the matter with *you*?" I screamed back at him. "You think you can do whatever you want? That every-one's just going to cater to you, because that's what's al-ways happened?"

"Whoa." Wex put his hands out to grab me by the shoulders. I threw my own hands up and stepped back. "What's happening right now?" he asked. "Where is this coming from?"

I tried to focus, but it was no good. My thoughts were all over the place. I didn't want to be here. It was all a mistake. But the words kept coming anyway.

"You and Anna just took yourselves out of the picture, like it didn't matter. Like *I* didn't matter," I said. "And then just 'cause that wasn't enough, you fucked up the one other problem I really could have used your help with. I told you not to show that video to Mitch. Jesus! And the whole idea was yours to begin with. I never should have listened to you."

"You're right," Wexler said. "I'm really, *really* sorry about that. But . . . is this about Mitch? Or is this about me and Anna? What do you want?"

I realized then that Anna had probably told him some of this already. He knew it wasn't just about Mitch. We both knew.

"I *wanted* things to stay the same," I said idiotically.

I wanted us back. Us three.

I wanted Wex to be a better friend.

I wanted the same for myself.

"I don't know what I want," I said, and finally took a breath. Then another. "But I miss you guys."

I stood there, as out of words now as I had been overflowing with them a second ago. My head was throbbing. My eyes felt too big for their sockets.

Wex looked about as lost as I felt. "Can we just . . ." He squinted and ducked his head to see my face. "Actually, do you need to go to the ER? Again?"

I don't know how the tiny fraction of whatever was funny about that wedged its way in—maybe because we needed it to—but there was something about that word—*again*—that broke through everything else. I let out a snot-heavy laugh, but stopped just as fast because it hurt like hell.

Wex was laughing, too, and trying to stop.

"Maybe just some paper towels?" I asked.

"And some ice," he said, and headed toward the back door. "Sit tight. I'll just be a second."

"What are you doing here, anyway?" I asked.

"Covering your shift," he said.

"Oh. Right." That made sense. I didn't work there anymore.

"I'm going to call Anna to take you home, too."

"Hey," I said, and he stopped with one hand on the door. "Mitch is over, okay? That's on me, but don't—"

"It's done," he said. "I won't say anything to him. Except maybe that I'm sorry."

I had to trust Wex on that, because obviously I wasn't going inside myself.

But the fact was, I did trust him, as much as anyone. Still.

5:15

When Mom came home and found Anna and me at the kitchen table, with a bag of frozen peas on my face and wads of rust-stained paper towels and tissues littering the table, she responded about the way I might have expected.

"Oh . . . *no*. Are you all right?" she asked. "What the hell happened here?"

"I'm okay," I said. "I got into a fight."

"With who?"

"That guy Mitch," I said.

Mom dropped her stuff on the counter and came over to peel away the peas and take a look.

"You don't get into fights," she said.

"That's why I didn't do too well," I said. "Also, I got fired." It seemed worth just putting it all out there at once.

"What?"

"For fighting."

They say one lie leads to another, and I guess it's true. I could only hope it was worth it in the big picture, when I was away at Birch and could put all of this behind me.

"You've been back less than twenty-four hours," Mom said. "And you've managed to get in the first fight of your life *and* fired?"

"Well, to be fair, it happened all at once," Anna said.

Her hand was in mine, and I squeezed.

Mom put the bag back on my face and dragged the kitchen garbage over to sweep away the rest of the mess. I was going to be blowing dark red for a while now. I already knew that from experience.

"This is incredible," Mom said.

"Tell me about it," I said.

"No, *you* tell *me* about it," she said. "Really. Who gets their face smashed in twice in one summer?"

I resisted the urge to look away. I thought about my answer for a second.

And in some other corner of the universe, I told her everything, all the way from the beginning. I told her about what happened behind the restaurant that first night, and about how I didn't think she'd necessarily freak out or anything, but that I wasn't at all sure she'd have been okay keeping it from Dad, which was where the deal breaker had always been. I told her that even though it scared me to come clean, it seemed like the right time to do it, and that if she needed to tell Dad, I understood. And if he needed to insert himself into my existence in some new way because of it, then I guess that was just how it was going to be.

Except—nothing good was going to come from that.

So, no.

Instead, I thumbed at myself and answered her question another way.

"I do," I said. "Apparently."

"Unbelievable," Mom said.

"Yeah, well . . ." Anna gave me a smile and gently patted my cheek. "It couldn't happen to a nicer version than this one right here."

4:40

We all went swimming that Friday. There was a great spot on the river outside of town, where you had to hike in, but that usually meant we had it to ourselves.

Besides Anna, Wex, and me, Berylin, Lainie, Eddie, Tyson, Jamie, and Rose were all there, all afternoon. Someone had tied a rope to a tree by the water, and I got some amazing slow-motion shots of them all, and Wex got some of me, too.

Everything was subject to its own soundtrack now. I couldn't take a shot without thinking about what music might go over it, or where in the bigger picture of this whole movie project it might fit. I still had a few weeks to finish, and I was picking up steam as I went.

I had an official title now, too. I was going to call it *Long Shot*. As in, a camera manuever, but also as in, what are the odds?

I mean, say what you want about the life you get to lead, but it is, by definition, the rarest possible thing. It's what happened—which is to say, the exception to the otherwise infinite number of things that didn't.

So, yeah. *Long Shot*.

"All right, I'm out of here," I said. The sun was just starting to angle through the trees on its way down, and I had to be at work later. I was on the graveyard shift at the all-night diner in Starkville—bussing tables at the new shitty job I'd been lucky enough to find. But it meant I was the first one who had to leave.

"What are you guys doing tomorrow night?" I asked Wex.

"We're getting a room at the motel," he said. "But Sunday's good, if you're around."

"All right, well, have fun," I said. It was cool. I really could be glad for them now.

A little glad for them.

A little.

I was getting used to it.

"Wait! Just take one more shot," Anna said then. "The light's really great right now."

She was right. It was beautiful, and I framed them all up, lying on their stomachs in a row on the concrete pad of what I think used to be a bridge foundation.

"You guys look like little kids," I said.

"I still feel like a little kid most of the time," Lainie said, and kicked her feet up behind her.

"Right?" Rose said.

I took a slow pan of them, moving from face to face, loving the image for its own sake, but also for the light— that amazing, end-of-day light.

"I can't believe we're going to be gone in a month," I said, putting the camera away.

"I was just thinking the same thing," Berylin said. "I'm really going to miss you guys."

Anna put her head on Berylin's shoulder. "And I'm really going to miss Prospero's Pizza," she said.

Berylin smacked her on the arm, and Eddie scooped up Lainie and threw her in the river, while Tyson picked out some music and Wexler shot me a peace sign, all before I turned and took the path back toward our cars on the side of the road.

I knew this wasn't the last time I'd walk up that trail at the end of the day with a damp towel around my neck, but I did wonder how many more times it might happen before it was all over. Five times? Twice?

There was no way of knowing for sure. But the countdown was most definitely on.

Epilogue

12:13

I used my shoulder to open the door and stepped backward into room 301 of Bremen Hall, where I'd be living for the year. I was one of the first people in the dorm, as far as I could tell. I'd had my pick of carts when I showed up in a cab with everything I'd managed to lug onto the plane. The rest of my stuff was coming by mail, hopefully in a day or two.

I had my choice of beds, too. Not that there seemed to be much difference, so I randomly picked the one on the left and dropped my stuff there.

I went over to the window next and checked the view. It wasn't bad—not the worst or best that Bremen Hall had to offer. I could see straight down the row of other dorms, where people were coming and going, and moving in, and starting their new lives. It was weird to imagine how familiar it was all going to be before long. I wondered which of those random people out there might be future friends. Or enemies, for that matter.

"Hello?" I heard behind me.

I turned and saw my roommate standing in the door, holding a huge cardboard box and with a loaded cart behind him.

"Hey!" I went over to help him with his stuff. "Neerav?"

"I assume you're Chris," he said, and we shook hands around the box in his arms. I was still self-conscious about my nose, but if he noticed anything, he didn't let on.

"How was your summer?" I asked.

"Great, actually," he said. "I was definitely ready to get out of the city and come here, but I had a nice exit, if you know what I mean. Lots of parties, lots of fun, a little travel."

He seemed like he liked to talk a lot. Hopefully not too much.

"How about you?" he asked.

"Not exactly the summer I was expecting," I said. "Actually, it was kind of weird, to be honest."

"Good weird, or bad weird?" he asked.

"A little of both, I guess."

He threw a carton onto the desk opposite mine and started pulling out what looked like a well-organized book collection. "Sounds like there's a story in there somewhere."

"There is," I said. "More than one, in fact. I'll have to tell you about it sometime."

Acknowledgments

This book took an extra-scenic route on the way to its own existence, and accordingly, I have a crazy-long list of people to thank for their help.

My agent, Michael Bourret, believed in this story before it was even half written. Then he shepherded it (and me) through the rest of the writing process with his particular brand of clear-eyed and unwavering optimism. He also assured me that my editor on this project, Kate Sullivan at Delacorte Press, is one of the best in the business, and he was right. Kate tolerated my nonsense with a sense of humor and a superhuman patience, long before she even started to dig in and make this book better than it ever would have been without her input. I want to be as smart as Kate when I grow up—and as lucky as she is, too, for landing an assistant as insightful and easy to work with as Alexandra Hightower. If anyone out there enjoys this book, it is in large part thanks to those three people.

Thanks also to my critique group: Barbara Gregorich, Jan Donley, Joe Nusbaum, Vicki Hayes, and Ruth Horowitz.

Their collective thumbprint is all over this story. Maybe even more important, they've provided me with a supportive community of peers who care, demonstrably, about one another's success, which is a rare and essential thing for a writer.

While I'm at it, I have to add an extra thank you to Ruth Horowitz. Nobody lived inside my brain through the completion of this book more than she did; nobody showed greater enthusiasm for what I was trying to do; and nobody helped me remember what I loved about writing this story as much as Ruth did, just when I needed it most.

And speaking of muses—this book deals in part with the seemingly random moments of great good fortune that happen in life, sometimes in the form of newfound love that we never thought we'd be lucky enough to find. There's a reason I have it in me to write about such things, and that reason is embodied in my husband, Jonathan. How lucky am I? That lucky.

Finally, this story took me into all kinds of research corners that I never would have otherwise reached into, which is itself one of the pleasures of writing. And it was in those various corners that I found some extreme generosity of spirit, not to mention some really smart and insightful people.

Thank you to the folks who helped me understand the world of physics and physicists and round out my layman's understanding of such things: Peter Pearson (who brings funny-smart to a whole new level); Luke Donforth and Denise Fontaine at the University of Vermont; William Karstens at Saint Michael's College; and Jim and Amber Lough.

Thanks also to those who so willingly shared their thoughts on faith, quite often in deeply considered and personal terms that went well beyond anything I'd originally hoped to gain from such conversations: Rebecca Anderson, Della Bowen St. Arnold, Jason Emery, Cyndy Craft, Nancy Thayer, and Kenney Irish.

Several professionals in the field of addiction and drug counseling were equally generous with their time, as well as with their insights to my character's particular situation. Thank you to Mandy Neeble-Diamond, Keenan Diamond, Sara Mason, Vicki Colvin, and Brian Townsend for that. Also to the young people who were brave enough to speak with me from their own experience: Chris, Eva, Ruby, Clint, Dan, and Jeff . . . thank you!

Lastly, a book like this doesn't happen without generating a Miscellaneous/Other list, and for that I have the following friends, acquaintances, and experts to thank for the information they gave, the pages they critiqued, the insights they offered, and/or whatever else I might be (okay, probably am) forgetting: Daniel Daltry, Olivia Taylor-Butler, Elizabeth Bluemle, Carolyn Walsh Powers, Ry Pearson, Charlotte Walsh, Steve Radigan, Dave Berman, Kate O'Neill, Valerie Hurley, and Elise Broach.

ABOUT THE AUTHOR

Chris Tebbetts is the *New York Times* bestselling coauthor of James Patterson's Middle School series. Originally from Yellow Springs, Ohio, Tebbetts lives and writes in Vermont. You can find him online at christebbetts.com and on Twitter and Instagram at @christebbetts.